THE BEST CHRISTMAS EVER

For my mum. My editor, my supporter, my best friend.
A better mum than any I could possibly write.

CONTENTS

Title Page

Copyright

Dedication

CHAPTER ONE   1

CHAPTER TWO   5

CHAPTER THREE   12

CHAPTER FOUR   15

CHAPTER FIVE   18

CHAPTER SIX   26

CHAPTER SEVEN   55

CHAPTER EIGHT   61

CHAPTER NINE   86

CHAPTER TEN   92

CHAPTER ELEVEN   96

CHAPTER TWELVE   110

CHAPTER THIRTEEN   114

Trouble in Tartan: CHAPTER ONE   118

Afterword   127

Books In This Series   129

CHAPTER ONE

Thirteen weeks until Christmas

Lee Davis had always been organised. As a child, she'd made lists to organise her dolls, made homework diaries well before she'd ever been assigned homework, and often reminded her mum and younger sister about appointments and plans. She loved to know what was going to happen and when - and that was possibly why everyone had been so shocked when, almost two years ago, she had started her life again in the rural town of Totnes, Devon.

Of course, there had been rather a shocking catalyst to that event, which had made her jump so far out of her comfort zone. Walking in on her husband, Nathan, sleeping with a blonde he'd met at work had finished their marriage, and made Shirley reconsider everything she'd ever known.

But despite a few spontaneous decisions - the trip to Totnes, buying a café, falling in love, having a baby - at heart, she still loved organising. And so when she had set out to plan her wedding to James, the gorgeous policeman who had stolen her heart and fathered her baby, she had set to it with a fresh notebook and a great deal of excitement.

And yet…

Somehow, everything seemed to be taking a lot longer than planned. She found herself putting off tasks that she should have completed, or debating decisions for far longer than they needed. Should she have a white dress? Was it ridiculous to have four bridesmaids the second time around? Who on earth would walk her down the aisle?

She had never expected planning the wedding to the love of her life to be so complicated.

"Do you need any help?" Beth, Lee's younger sister, asked one night over the phone.

"No, it's all fine," Lee lied. They had spent a long while discussing Beth's new love interest, who Lee couldn't wait to meet, and so it had taken quite a while for the conversation to come round to the wedding.

"Are you sure? I was expecting to be inundated with dress fittings and maid-of-honour duties by now; it's only three months to go! You definitely have got your dress?"

"Yes, yes, I told you when you were round that I had it!"

"Hmmm. Not sure I'll believe that 'til I see it."

"Well you won't be seeing it until the wedding day, so I guess I'll have to cope with your disbelief!" Privately, Lee wasn't too sure whether she was going to keep the dress. She'd fallen in love with it when she'd seen it in the little bridal shop round the corner from the café she owned in Totnes. She'd only gone in on a whim, with a rare bit of time without her almost one-year-old daughter Holly or her husband-to-be, and had certainly not expected to buy a dress in the first shop she'd looked in.

But there it had been; hanging towards the back of the shop, on sale and in Lee's size. That alone seemed like a sign. It was white satin, very simple, with a scooped neck-line and the most beautiful red satin trim around the train. It was perfect - the red would fit her Christmas wedding theme, and when she tried it on, she knew she just had to have it. She told James she'd bought it, although of course he wasn't allowed to see it, and had let Beth and her mum know, when they'd asked - but it was hung in the back of her wardrobe, not to be seen by anyone until the big day.

It was about a week after she'd bought it that she'd started to have doubts. When she got it out of the ward-robe to take another look, she worried it was too much; too beautiful, too white, too exquisite to be a second wedding dress. Outside of the luxury of the shop, it seemed much more decadent, and she found worries creeping in that their guests might not feel she should be wearing some-thing so beautiful.

These worries had not been voiced to anyone; she knew Beth would say she was being ridiculous. James would re-assure her - but this was only his first wedding, and she didn't really like to discuss her first failed marriage more than she had to. She certainly didn't want him to feel guilty about their big day - and he deserved to have the big white wedding too.

So she took to sighing every time she looked at the dress - but not actually making any decisions either way about whether she would wear it.

"Lee? Are you even listening?" Her sister's voice on the other end of the line brought her back to reality.

"Sorry Beth. Yeah, I am, carry on…"

CHAPTER TWO

Twelve weeks until Christmas

"Mama! Mama!" It was the way most of Lee's days started, and although it was still dark outside, her daughter was clearly ready to start the day. She rolled over in bed to the cold side and sighed; James had left very early for his shift, so she wouldn't be seeing him until later in the day.

"Coming!" she shouted, and when she entered her daughter's bedroom, Holly was stood up in her cot, holding the bars and grinning, curly brown hair all over the place. She definitely had her hair and her eyes from her dad; as well as her laid back attitude, Lee thought.

"Morning beautiful girl," she said, lifting her out of the cot and setting her down on the floor, double checking the stair gate was closed. After an accident a few weeks previously involving a large bump to Holly's head where she'd rolled into the kitchen island, Lee was being extra careful with stair gates and baby-proofing - especially since she was now tentatively cruising whenever she could pull herself up onto the furniture.

The usual routine of dressing, breakfast and some cartoons ensued. Rain battered the windows, and Lee couldn't help but think back to the similarly miserable, wet day when she had walked in and found her husband with another woman. Such a terrible day, that had turned her life upside down and made her question so many things - and yet in some ways, perhaps a hidden blessing. Without that terrible, heart-breaking event, she would never have moved to Totnes, nor met James, or had Holly. Her life would be totally unrecognisable - and would she have been happier? She struggled to imagine how she could be. This felt like it was where she was meant to be, who she was meant to be - her happily ever after, as her sister put it.

A walk was out of the question, so Lee got out the building blocks and began building with Holly. That afternoon, when James got home, she knew she had a few cases to look over, so she made the most of the time with her daughter now. As much as she loved running the café, practising law and being a mother, sometimes it felt like she was being pulled in lots of different directions.

When the phone rang at eleven, Lee only just got to it in time - she had just finished putting Holly down for her morning nap. She was slightly out of breath from dashing down the stairs, and when she heard the voice on the other end, it nearly made her stop breathing all together.

"Hi, Lee."

It was a voice she hadn't heard for over a year, a voice she had not expected to hear again.

"Lee?"

"Nathan?"

A pause; she didn't need to ask. She knew exactly who it was. You couldn't be married to someone for years and not recognise their voice.

"How are you?" he asked, strangely polite.

"Fine," she answered, her mind racing at why he might be getting in touch with her. She didn't offer any more; he had rung, he could explain why he was calling, or ask if he had something he wanted to know.

"Good, good. I heard you're getting married?"

Lee wondered who would have told him that - as far as she knew, anyone she was in contact with was no longer in contact with him. They hadn't particularly had any mutual friends, and her family certainly had no interest in maintaining contact with the man who had broken her heart and her marriage.

"Yes," she said, then curiosity got the better of her. "How did you know?"

"I ran into Gemma Phillips," he said. "From your old law firm."

"Ah." She had invited her former colleagues, both of whom had said they would come, and she guessed there was no reason for them to keep the information from him, if they saw him.

"Congratulations."

The conversation was painfully stilted, and she wished he would just get to the point of why he had rung.

"Thank you."

Silence; she would wait. She was not going to fill the awkward silence to make him feel more comfortable; he could do that.

"You're probably wondering why I rang…"

"Yes, I am." She was surprised at how rude she was able to be.

"Emily is pregnant."

"And Emily is?" She was pretty sure she could guess, but didn't want to make the presumption. Besides, he sounded awkward, and she thought he deserved to.

"My…girlfriend."

"Ah. The blonde?"

"No…"

She almost laughed, but there wasn't really anything funny. The woman he'd cheated with wasn't even some love of his life, wasn't the woman he would end up with - she was just a fling, and now another woman was in the mix.

"Congratulations."

"I'm not ready to be a father…"

She sighed. "Nathan, I don't understand why you're ringing me. We don't exactly have a soul-baring relationship, so I don't know why you're telling me this."

She thought her tone might make him hang up - hoped as much, even - but she didn't seem to be able to shake him that easily.

"We were married five years, Lee, and I don't know who else to tell…"

"Frankly, you should have thought about that."

"I should have done." That surprised her; even when he'd been caught, he'd never particularly admitted any fault. "It was a huge mistake, Lee - I made a huge mistake. And now I'm with someone I don't love, and she's pregnant with my baby."

Lee was very proud of herself for not suggesting that it was karma. She took a deep breath, and sank into the sofa cushions, phone pressed to her ear and baby monitor in the other hand.

"You wouldn't have been ready to have a baby with me, either - and that would have ended our marriage. One way or another, we weren't destined to grow old together, Nathan."

"How can you be so cold about it?"

She tried not to take that as an insult. "I've moved on, Nathan. I can look back and not feel heartbroken because I have a wonderful daughter and am about to marry the man I love. I'm sorry you're not in the same position." She thought that she probably even meant that; she had hated him for what he'd done, but now she didn't feel any emotion as strong as hate towards him. In fact, hearing him on the other end of the phone, what she mainly felt was pity - even though he had brought it on himself. She hoped the child would not be raised as the burden he was so obviously feeling it was at present.

"What if you were the one I was meant to grow old with, Lee?"

"Then you wouldn't have cheated your way through the doctors and nurses you work with." She was pleased with herself for being so blunt - and that the words no longer made her chest ache.

He didn't have a response for that, it seemed, and when silence had reigned for longer than it was comfortable, Lee spoke again. "Either make a go of it with her, or don't - but that baby will be part of your life now, and there's no escaping from it. You need to focus on what's best for the baby - try not to be selfish, Nathan."

"I shouldn't have messed things up with you, Lee," he said again, but Lee had no answer for him this time.

"Goodbye, Nate. Good luck." She put the phone down without waiting for a response, and let out a sigh. What a conversation...

"You'll never guess who called today," Lee said to James that evening as he cooked dinner and she helped Holly to cover a piece of paper in random crayon scribblings.

James raised his eyebrows in anticipation, stirring something delicious-smelling on the hob.

"Nathan."

"What did he want, after all this time?" The two had never met - something which Lee was very happy about - but she had always been honest with him about any contact from her ex-husband. After all, when they had got together she had been separated from Nathan, but not yet divorced. That had been why she had been so reluctant to get together with James, even though every fibre of her body had been willing her to.

"To tell me he's going to be a father. And to lament past mistakes…" She didn't go into too much detail, not wanting Holly to hear anything about the situation, but James seemed to get the gist.

He ran a hand through his curly brown hair, and fixed his eyes on hers. "Does he know you're getting married?"

"He's heard, apparently. He apologised, said it was a huge mistake - and then was surprised I was cold about it all!"

James smiled, looking visibly relieved. "As long as he doesn't think he has any hope of winning you back," he said.

Lee got up from the table and put her arm around his waist, resting her head on his shoulder. "You are the man I will grow old with, James Knight. Don't worry about that."

He pressed his lips against hers and grinned. "I love you."

CHAPTER THREE

Eleven weeks until Christmas

James Knight rarely shopped for clothes. It wasn't something he particularly enjoyed, and considering he was in uniform so often, he didn't need a particularly large range of clothes. Despite his lack of enthusiasm for shopping, he wasn't dreading today's shopping trip too much, and that was because it was to pick out the suits for his wedding.

He'd been in this position once before, with a woman who he thought would be the one he settled down with and spend the rest of his life with. They had picked suits and dresses, paid for the flowers, organised the caterers - and then she'd decided that their life was not what she wanted. She didn't want the small town, and she didn't want James.

Not this time. He was sure, as sure as he'd ever been about anything, that he would grow old and grey with Lee. They had their daughter, and perhaps they'd have another - or maybe not. But his world was wherever they were, and anything that brought them closer to being legally wed was something he was happy to do.

His brother, Jack, was waiting outside the shop, which was already bedecked in Christmas lights and tinsel. They greeted with a brief hug, and as they always did, asked about each other's children, who were only a few months apart in age.

"Can't shut Jasper up," Jack said with a grin. "Like his mother - loves to talk!"

"It's walking at the minute with Holly," James said. "Pulls herself up on every surface, and then you're chasing after her when she lets go, worried she's going to fall over!"

They were greeted in the shop by a young woman of twenty or so, who showed them a few different styles of suits they could try on.

"Does Lee have an opinion on which style you should have?" Jack, who would be his best man, asked. Although he tended to go by his full name of John these days, James had difficulty thinking of him as anything other than 'Jack', as that was what they had always called him as children. Back then, he had only been 'John' when he was in trouble!

"She said my choice, which to be honest is terrifying." He ran a hand through his curly hair with a grin. "I feel like there's definitely a right and a wrong choice."

Jack laughed. "Probably. But it's red ties, right?"

"Cravats, I think! Red, and red pocket squares - to go with the bridesmaids' dresses."

"Well that's simple enough. Here, try on some of these jackets and see which you like."

James rolled his eyes, and then did as his big brother told him.

"You feeling nervous about the wedding, then?" Jack asked, trying on a jacket himself.

"Not really," James said. "I mean, I'm not all that keen on being watched by a load of people, but the actual getting married part - no."

"No second thoughts?" Jack teased.

"Absolutely none. I hope Lee feels the same…"

Jack paused in his attempts to do up a cravat. "What makes you say that?"

James didn't quite meet his eye as he voiced the concern that he hadn't shared with anyone else. "I don't know. She just doesn't seem so excited about Christmas this year - and it's her favourite time of the year, normally. She's a bit obsessed with all things festive!"

"It's still a bit early for Christmas!" he said with a laugh. "Anyway, maybe she's just focussing on the wedding instead?" Jack suggested.

"Maybe. I can't help thinking she's not as excited about that. Maybe because she's done it before…"

"James, she loves you. She wants to be married to you. If you think she's not as excited about it, maybe you should ask her why? Because I don't think it's second thoughts - not for a moment."

James smiled. "Thanks, Jack. Right, I think this is the best one - what do you think?"

CHAPTER FOUR

Ten weeks until Christmas

"You're not going to make me wear some massive, frilly, pink confection are you?" Gina said with a wicked grin. "When I agreed to be bridesmaid, I did say no ridiculous dresses…"

"Well it is my wedding," Lee said to her friend and colleague, Gina. She laughed; "But no, that was not my plan. In fact, since there is no way I can pick something to all your tastes, I was just going to let you pick your own. As long as it's red!"

Gina's eyes lit up. "Sounds like a great plan! I'll get looking straight away…" They were working together in the café that day, which was quite a rare occurrence. When Lee had moved to Totnes almost two years previously, it had been Gina's spare room where she had first lived. When she'd bought the café, it had made sense to offer Gina a job - and although Gina was so different to Lee, they had become firm friends very quickly. Back then, they had worked together almost every day, but with Lee's pregnancy, law work, and the fact that the café was turning over a decent profit, they no longer worked there every hour under the sun. Still, Lee enjoyed the days when they did end up there together - although since Gina was currently dating Tom, their other employee, she wondered which days Gina preferred.

It was a quiet spell in the café, and so as Lee began wiping down surfaces, Gina whipped out her phone and started her search, occasionally thrusting it in front of Lee's face to see what she thought of the option. Lee was pleased that they were all suitably bridesmaid-esque; she didn't want to have to say no to anything outlandish, but she was fairly sure Gina knew the areas where their tastes diverged.

"Is there anything else wedding-wise you need me to do?" Gina asked as they made coffees side by side later that day. "I've never been a bridesmaid before, not really sure what you want me to do…"

Lee smiled. "I think it's all under control, to be honest. Beth is organising a hen do - although I said I didn't need one! That terrifies me a little bit…"

"You always make your sister out to be so wild," Gina said. "I think I'll have to get to know her better!"

"She's wild compared to me, I guess - maybe not compared to you!"

"I'm positively tame these days," Gina replied. "Besides, I've never upped sticks and bought a café, have I!"

"My one wild act and I'll never hear the end of it…"

The dresses for James' sister, her wife and John's wife were simpler; although she gave them the option to choose for themselves, they were all very happy to go with whatever Lee liked, and so she emailed them over a few options to choose from while she was meant to be working on a case. She was finding it hard, between the café, Holly and the law firm, not to mention actually spending time with James, to put the finishing touches to this wedding - and the butterflies about people judging her were still there every time she looked at her own dress.

She presumed the three had talked, for they all agreed on the same dress, which certainly made Lee's life a little easier. She ordered it in the sizes requested, and arranged for them to come over later in the week, to try them on, and, of course, to see their niece. James barely got a look-in these days!

She hoped to go shopping with her sister to find the right dress; it would be nice to spend some time together. Although she'd finally met her mystery man, it seemed that things had not worked out between them; he had moved for work to Edinburgh, and Beth seemed more miserable than Lee could remember ever seeing her. It would do them good to enjoy a girly day shopping - and perhaps take Beth's mind off her current heartache.

CHAPTER FIVE

Nine weeks until Christmas

The city centre was bustling, and although Halloween wasn't quite upon them yet, Christmas decorations were in almost every shop. They weaved their way through families, couples and one particularly raucous hen party - which gave Lee a chance to remind Beth that her own hen party was to be sedate with absolutely no strippers - towards the first dress shop Lee had researched. They knew they were looking for fancy, and they knew they were looking for red - but other than that, they weren't too sure. Lee had taken photos of the dresses her sisters-in-law and Gina had chosen, but she wasn't too worried about them 'matching' - as long as they were all red, and no-one was wearing anything so indecent it would distract from the ceremony, she thought it would all look lovely. Holly was taking her morning nap strapped in the pushchair, and although it was difficult pushing it through shop doorways, she was glad she had brought it - much easier than carrying a sleepy almost-one-year-old around a busy city centre.

Beth pulled out a red tutu-ed number with a strapless top, and was rewarded with an expression from Lee that made her crack up, although they both pretended not to be laughing when the shop assistant came to ask them if they needed any help. Once they'd explained what they were looking for, she'd pulled out almost every red dress in the store, but none were quite what Beth was thinking. Lee could have said she were being fussy, but she agreed with her sister - none were quite wow enough for a wedding.

The next shop felt a little more relaxed, and Lee was pleased that there were no dresses Beth could laugh about here. They picked out three different red dresses, and while Lee stood outside the changing room with the pushchair, Beth tried them all on. The first was far too short - and she was pleased Beth agreed - and the second just fitted weirdly, giving Beth an unattractive silhouette that she definitely didn't deserve. The third, however, fit like a glove. It had a halter neckline and went in at the waist, skimming Beth's hips and stopping just below the knee, which complimented her short stature perfectly.

"It's beautiful, Beth," Lee said with a grin. "And very you."

Beth looked in the mirror, spinning round and looking back at herself over her shoulder. "I shan't have a date to impress," she said with a sigh. "But I do think it looks pretty good."

Lee grinned. "Is it the one?"

Beth rolled her eyes. "I'm not sure you get 'the one' with a bridesmaid dress like you do a wedding dress - but I would say it's a pretty strong contender. But the day is still young... let's ask them to put it behind the counter, and then if there's nothing better then we know it's the one."

Lee nodded; "Your wish is my command," she said. This trip was as much to cheer Beth up in her post-Caspian funk as it was about finding dresses. Holly was beginning to stir, and Lee glanced at her watch. "I reckon we've got time for one quick shop - then we need to find somewhere for lunch or we'll have a grumpy child on our hands!"

After a messy lunch in a luckily quiet café, Lee and Beth loaded up on some caffeine to help continue their shopping trip. Whether or not the bridesmaid dress was 'the one', they still had to get some shoes to go with it; Lee also needed to pick up Holly's flower girl dress, which was waiting in the shop for her.

They chatted about the wedding, about Lee's crazy commitment to have the whole family over for Christmas, just three days after their wedding - but the topic of Caspian, Beth's ex, did not come up. Had Beth wanted to talk about it, Lee would've been happy to - but it seemed like she wanted to distract herself from thinking about him, so Lee didn't bring it up. She hated seeing her sister so upset about a man; it had been a long time since she had seen her fall for someone so hard, and the fact that it hadn't worked out when everything seemed so perfect made Lee's heart hurt for her sister.

"Ooh, let's go in here," Beth said, grabbing Lee's hand and dragging her - and the pushchair - into a little vintage dress shop. The walls were packed with dresses of all shapes, sizes and colours, and Lee couldn't get any further than just inside the doorway with the pram. Beth had already disappeared into the treasure trove of clothing, and Lee rolled her eyes with a smile. Just like Beth to forget that it wasn't quite so easy for Lee to disappear into a tiny shop. She glanced around, and decided to lift Holly onto her hip and leave the pram in the corner where it was, hoping she could keep an eye on it.

"This is perfect for you," Beth said, pulling out an emerald green twenties-style dress. "Way too long for me, but perfect for you."

"It is gorgeous," Lee said, stroking her fingers down the delicate material. "What a stunning colour."

"Try it on!"

"When would I wear it?" Lee said.

"Who cares! On your honeymoon, whenever you get round to having one. Or on a night out! It's gorgeous - go on, try it on. I'll take Holly - yes, yes, and I'll keep an eye on the pram."

Lee wriggled out of her jeans and top and glanced at the dress. It was beautiful; and it had been a long time since she'd treated herself to fancy clothes - wedding dress excluded. Since having Holly, she didn't feel so confident in her own skin - and many items in her wardrobe still felt a little tight across the stomach. She didn't like to look at herself for very long in the mirror, especially without clothes on, and so she slipped the dress on quickly and glanced at her reflection. She grinned; it skimmed her stomach, making it look a lot flatter, and hung off her shoulders in a way that may her neck look longer and her whole body look slimmer. She reached round and looked at the tag; it was a little pricier than she was hoping, but she didn't think it was too crazy, and the way it made her feel meant she was convinced it was meant to be hers.

Once she'd redressed and carefully folded the dress over

her arm, she exited to find Beth trying on some very Dorothy-esque sparkly red shoes, with Holly clapping appreciatively.

"They're lovely," Lee said.

"Aren't they! What do you think - they'd go so well with the dress we put back, don't you think?"

"Perfect," Lee said. "I'll get them - I can't resist this dress!"

"Yay!" Beth said with a grin. "Although you don't have to buy these, I'll get them."

"Don't be silly, they're for my wedding. We'd best make sure we get back and get that dress though, before they sell it to someone else!"

Having picked up Holly's dress - red with a white net skirt underneath that made it puff up, and a red tartan sash around the middle - and stopped in a men's store to buy James a blue jumper Lee had seen in the window, they bought Beth's dress and glanced at the clock.

"I'm exhausted," Lee said, feeling a little jealous of Holly who was happily back asleep in her pram.

"One more shop," Beth said. "I think we should get a red tartan sash for me too - to match Holly. What do you think?" She seemed excited by the idea, and Lee thought it was cute, so off they trudged, bags of clothes beneath the pram and in desperate need of some more coffee.

"Happy birthday to you," they sang, loudly and out of tune but with much enthusiasm. "Happy birthday to you!" The birthday girl sat in a rainbow dress with a tutu skirt, looking a little bemused at the song, the candle coming towards her and her crying mother. "Happy birthday dear Holly, happy birthday to you." A cheer went up from the assembled family and friends, and James held the cake in front of Holly - although away from her wispy hair.

"Blow out the candle, darling!" he said, and with some help from Lee and James, and another loud cheer, the candle was extinguished.

Holly promptly burst into tears.

While Holly was comforted by her mother, whose own tears at her daughter turning one had been leaking from her eyes on and off all day, Beth whisked away the cake to find a knife from behind the counter. When Lee had decided to throw a first birthday party for her daughter, the café had seemed the obvious location, and with the amount of family who'd shown up, it was a good job they had a decent sized space.

Beth had been tasked with taking photographs, and so she attempted to capture some posed and some candid shots of the little family groups, getting Holly in with them as often as possible - although, as nap time edged ever closer, her mood became less sunny. She was pleased to catch a shot of her mum playing with Holly, since photos of the two of them always seemed a little awkward, and another of her sat with her cousin Jasper among a pile of building blocks.

"I can't believe she's one already," Lee said, wiping her

eyes for the millionth time and coming to stand next to Beth. "I feel like it was five minutes ago I was throwing up on the street, not knowing I was pregnant!"

"Way too much information," Beth said with a grin, nevertheless putting down the slice of cake she was eating. "But it has gone really fast. All of it, really. It doesn't seem long ago you were living in Bristol with *him*, and I was in Exeter. And now look at us. You're getting married, you have a one-year-old daughter, a million businesses…"

Lee laughed and tapped her sister playfully on the arm. "Not a million!" she said. "Two. That's all."

"Yeah, that's all. And I… I have a job. And I live in Dartmouth."

"And you've written a book!" Lee said. "That's huge."

Beth nodded. "I guess. I thought things were all going to work out for me, I guess… like they did for you."

Lee threw her arm around her sister and gave her a squeeze. "They will do. I'm sure of it. And even though things aren't perfect, you're happier than you were in Exeter, aren't you?"

Beth thought for a moment, before nodding. "Yes. Yes, I'm definitely happier."

The nights continued to darken earlier and earlier, and with Holly's first birthday gone, Halloween was hot on its heels. Even though it hadn't been something Lee and Beth had ever particularly celebrated as kids, with a cute toddler to dress up this year it felt different. Beth came over that afternoon, with a witch's costume that unfortunately made Holly cry for a good ten minutes, before she realised it was her aunt underneath it. Lee had gone for a much friendlier looking 'Good Witch of the West' costume, with James joining in as the scarecrow - both of which made Holly laugh.

"Favouritism," Beth muttered as they dressed Holly in the Toto the dog costume Lee had excitedly ordered a few weeks previously.

Beth took photos of them together as a family, and as much as she enjoyed the trick-or-treating with the neighbours, who oohed and ahhed at how cute Holly was, she couldn't help but feel a little left out. It wasn't anyone's fault; they just had their little family, and she was on the fringes of it. Part of it, but not at the core - and that was a strange kind of loneliness that she wasn't sure she'd been aware of before.

CHAPTER SIX

Six weeks until Christmas

There were six weeks ago until Christmas and only slightly less until Lee and James's Christmas wedding. Things seemed to have been going according to plan, although Lee was still struggling to find the Christmas spirit she normally had in abundance.

As November drew to a close, the air turned much colder, although Lee didn't hold out much hope for snow. The first year she'd been here they'd had a white Christmas - something which she thought the residents would talk about for years to come. Snow this close to the seaside was fairly rare; at most, Dartmoor would get a dusting.

Lee was working a shift in a cafe that day and she tried to muster up some Christmas spirit for a day that would be filled with making Christmas drinks and discussing people's Christmas shopping plans. On the way out of the door, she paused to kiss Holly and James goodbye.

"Are you sure everything's alright?" James asked, and Lee nodded.

"Just busy," she said. "Christmas and a wedding in the same week - what were we thinking?" James paused. Lee's hand was still on the door handle, ready to leave, and it was just as she opened it that he spoke again.

"And you're sure about the wedding?"

"What do you mean?" Lee asked, abandoning the door handle and moving to put her hand across his.

"This isn't the time to discuss it," James said. "Sorry - it's just that... you don't seem that thrilled about it all, I guess."

Lee felt her heart jump. The hurt look in his eye made her want to stop and reassure him, but she was running late for work - and there were more complicated issues than could be discussed in five minutes; her own insecurities were hard to shake off.

"I'm thrilled to be marrying you," she said, pressing her lips to his and feeling his respond instantly. "I'm sorry if I ever made you doubt that."

"I love you."

"I love you too." And with that she was out the door, knowing that she would need to explain her worries to him soon enough - otherwise he'd be convinced she didn't want to marry him, and nothing could be further from the truth.

She was ten minutes late in the end, although Gina had already opened up and was serving a few customers who needed their early morning, pre-work coffee fix.

"Sorry," Lee said. "Didn't mean to be late!"

"No worries, you know it's never that busy 'til a bit later on. You could have had a lie-in!"

"With a one-year-old!" Lee laughed. "Never happens."

"There's a guy over in the corner who wanted to see you," Gina said in a whisper, glancing over to a table in the corner with two chairs. Lee surreptitiously tried to look to where Gina had indicated; a thin man with a grey beard and short grey hair sat sipping a cup of tea.

"Did he say who he was?"

Gina shook her head. "Just asked for 'Shirley' - took me a second to figure out who he meant!"

Lee furrowed her brow. Very few people in her life knew her as Shirley, let alone called her it.

"Hello," she said, once she had put on her apron and made her way over to the man. "I'm Lee - Shirley - Davis. Can I help?"

He surveyed her as he put down his cup of tea, and she was sure she recognised him - even more so when he smiled.

"Shirley - it's me, Ted. Your dad."

"Dad?" Lee didn't know what to say. Of course, now he said who he was, she could see it in his face; could tell why she had recognised him. But it had been a very long time since she had seen him, and back then he had not been grey, and had weighed a fair amount more than he did now.

"I'm sorry to just turn up like this," he said, when Lee did not offer any other words. "And I know you need to work."

Lee nodded, without finding any words.

"Can I wait for you to have a break?" he asked. "I'll leave if someone wants the table. Or if you don't want me to stay…"

"You can stay." Lee had finally found her voice, although her mind was racing. "I don't known when I'll have some time..."

"That's fine," Ted said with a smile. "The tea's lovely."

She nodded, and made her way back to the counter. She wanted to tell someone, and her immediate thought was to message Beth. But Beth was going through her own difficulties with Caspian, and this seemed like one thing too many for her to deal with right now. Her mum? No - the handful of times her father had been mentioned over the last twenty-odd years, his name had never been uttered favourably, and it seemed like time had never healed the wound. Not that she could blame her mum; her dad had run off with his secretary and left her to raise two young girls. After all, Lee had been on the same side of a cheating husband as her mum - and that had hurt her immeasurably, even without children involved. She didn't think she would have been so calm about the whole situation now if Nate had left her with young children to bring up alone.

She watched him for a moment as he sipped his tea and perused a newspaper. It felt unreal, to look upon a father that she had not seen since she was six years old, casually sat in her cafe. How had he found her? Why had he found her? They had not heard anything from him in years; the odd birthday or Christmas gift when they were children, but not much since they had grown. He had not been at Lee's first wedding; she didn't even know if he had been aware she was getting married. She'd asked her mum to send the invite, but Tina never heard back, and hadn't been sure she even had the right address - and so he quite possibly never knew.

"So?" Gina asked, after she'd finished serving a regular customer. "Who's the silver fox?"

"My dad," Lee said, finding the words a little alien to speak. She so rarely spoke of him, or even thought about him these days.

"I didn't know you had a dad," Gina said, wiping crumbs from the counter top. "Well - you know what I mean."

"I haven't seen him since I was a kid."

"Oh. What does he want?"

Lee sighed. "Not a clue."

"Don't you want to find out?"

"I'm not sure..."

It was well over an hour later when Lee finally ran out of jobs she felt had to be done and had no excuse but to go and sit with her father. Gina assured her she was fine alone, and so Lee made herself a coffee and took it over to the table, along with another cup of tea and a couple of scones.

"Sorry to keep you so long," she said, knowing her tone was stiff and formal, but not sure how to make it any other way. She wished James were here; even without knowing much about the situation, she was sure he'd know the right things to say.

"No problem. I did turn up out of the blue..."

"How did you find me?" Lee asked. "Sorry, that was a bit

blunt, I meant-"

"A bit of internet stalking I'm afraid," he said with a smile. "There was an article in the local newspaper about you taking over this place, so I thought I'd swing by…"

"Where are you living now?" Lee asked, confused by how on earth he could 'swing by'.

"Well," Ted said, looking a tad sheepish. "London. So I guess 'swing by' is a bit of a stretch."

Lee let out a sharp laugh. "It is a bit!"

"You look wonderfully well, Shirley."

"You look very well yourself."

"It's been so long…"

Lee nodded. "So why now?"

"I don't know what your mum's said to you about me, over the years…"

"Not much," Lee said, a little more sharply than she planned to.

Ted gave a sad smile. "I don't want to drag up old history. But my not seeing you all these years has not been entirely my own choice."

Lee's hand stopped in mid-air, her cup halfway to her mouth. "What does that mean?"

"I didn't want to disappear from your lives - yours and Elizabeth's. But your mum asked me to stay away… and I'm afraid I complied." He smiled. "You know how your mum can be."

"I do…" Lee said, lowering her cup to the table without having taken a sip. "But I also know you walked out on her to be with your secretary, so I can't blame her entirely."

"I did," Ted said. "And I don't blame your mum for being angry, or hurt, or not wanting to have anything to do with me. But I do feel that I shouldn't have been kept away from you girls - and I shouldn't have let myself be kept away."

"So why now?" Lee repeated, giving her brain time to catch up. She'd always assumed her dad didn't want anything to do with them, not that he'd been asked not to. Actually, that wasn't just an assumption… she was pretty sure her mother had said it outright more than once. There was a lot there to mull over…

"I have to admit, I search your names quite a lot. Never got the guts up to actually get in touch though, not for a long time…" He smiled. "Anyway, I saw a marriage announcement."

"Ah." The announcement in the local gazette had not been Lee's idea, nor James's, but his mum had been so excited about the idea that Lee hadn't seen any harm in it. The locals round here liked to know what was going on, and they would have found out one way or another - there were no secrets in a town like Totnes.

"Congratulations," he said with a smile.

"Thank you."

"A police officer, it said."

"Yeah, James." She paused, and took a sip of her coffee. "Did you see the birth announcement too?" Another idea from James's mum - although how much of the local paper was available online, Lee wasn't sure. It wasn't something she had ever considered, until now.

By the look on Ted's face, that particular announcement had passed him by.

"I'm a grandad?" he said, his face lighting up, and Lee couldn't help but smile. She pulled out her phone and showed a recent picture of Holly, face covered in food and a grin on her lips.

"Holly. She was a year old in October."

His eyes were fixed to the photo as he replied. "She's beautiful."

"I agree, although I'm probably biased." She put her phone back in her pocket and drained the luke-warm coffee. "I'd better get back to work, I'm afraid." She had a lot to sort through in her mind, although she felt a definite softening of her feelings towards him.

"I'm staying in Salcombe," he said, finishing his tea. "Thought I'd spend a couple of days down here. Can-Can I see you again?"

She took a deep breath. "This is all very sudden, I wasn't expecting…

"I know, I know." He looked so hopeful, she couldn't find it in herself to disappoint him.

"But I guess so." He grinned, and pulling a pen from her apron pocket and a serviette from the table, Lee scribbled her number down. "Here," she said, handing it to him. "Message me tomorrow, and we'll work something out."

He stood, and leaned over as if to hug her, then seemed to think better of it and patted her arm awkwardly instead. "It's been lovely to see you, Shirley."

"Everyone calls me Lee," she said.

"Even your mother?"

Lee smiled at that. "No, everyone except her."

"Okay, Lee. And I'd love to see Elizabeth too, sometime, if that would be possible."

The cafe was filling up with lunchtime trade, and Lee could see Gina was getting swamped. "Tomorrow, okay? I'm not working then."

◆ ◆ ◆

James didn't bring up the morning's unfinished discussion when Lee got home, and she was so thrown by her father's impromptu visit that for a while after she walked through the door, the topic didn't even enter her mind.

They chatted over an early dinner about James' day with Holly and what time she'd napped, and it wasn't until she was safely tucked up in bed and finally snoring away softly that Lee remembered that they needed to finish that conversation - as well as discuss the appearance of her absentee father.

"Pour me a glass of wine, would you?" she called into the kitchen where James was finishing the washing up. "And come and sit with me!"

James appeared a few moments later, carrying two

glasses of red and a packet of peanuts. He grinned guiltily. "I'm all for eating together as a family, but the early dinners leave me starving the rest of the evening!"

"Hey, no judgment here." She grabbed a glass of wine and a handful of peanuts, then turned to face James on the sofa, crossing her legs in front of her. "So," she said.

"You're scaring me."

Lee smiled, and took hold of his hand. "I'm really sorry, James. I'm sorry if I've made you feel like you need to worry. You don't. I am all in and I want nothing more than to marry you."

James smiled, looking relieved, and ran his fingers across the back of her hand. "Phew," he said. "I've been worried, I have to admit. You don't exactly seem excited about the wedding - or Christmas. It's just not what I was expecting."

"I get that. And I'm not even sure I can explain it one hundred percent myself... but please believe me that I am excited and will most definitely be walking down that aisle on December 22nd."

James leant to press his lips to hers and she could taste the fruitiness of the wine on his tongue.

"I'm very pleased to hear that."

His fingers found her hair as he carefully held the wine glass in his other hand, and Lee gave herself over to the feeling. With two jobs and a one-year-old, it was a lot rarer than she would have liked to enjoy a glass of wine and the feel of her soon-to-be husband's lips on hers.

"I love you," she said, when his lips moved to her neck and her eyes fluttered closed.

"I love you too."

A moan escaped Lee's lips and she let James take the half-drunk glass of wine from her hand and place it carefully alongside his on the coffee table.

"Next month," he said, pulling her hand to lead her up the stairs. "You will be Mrs Knight, and I will be even happier than I am now."

Lee's eyes were fluttering closed, her limbs entangled in the sheets and her head resting on James' bare chest, when she remembered the other topic that needed to be discussed. She was too tired and her head too fuzzy to raise it now; it could wait until tomorrow. The most important issue had be settled; even if she couldn't quite explain why she wasn't as excited about the wedding as she should have been. Even if she couldn't bring herself to tell him of her fears about being judged on her second time down the aisle. But he knew that she loved him, knew that she would be his wife in a few short weeks - and that was all that mattered.

James was grinning as he passed her a coffee over the breakfast table the next morning, and she couldn't help but feel happy by his buoyant mood.

"Good morning, my love," he said, turning back to the hob. "As I don't need to be in until eleven, I'm making pancakes for breakfast."

Lee picked Holly up from where she had been colouring on the floor and gave her a kiss. "Pancakes! What lucky girls we are, hey?" Holly beamed and threw her arms roughly round Lee's neck. "How about some cartoons, princess? While mummy talks to daddy."

"Toons!" Holly said with a big grin. "Toons!"

When Lee reappeared in the kitchen, James had already begun a stack of pancakes on a plate next to the stove.

"So," she said. "You distracted me yesterday…"

He leant over to kiss her on the cheek. "A good distraction I hope!"

"The best," she said with a grin. "But I had something else I needed to talk to you about." She took a deep breath. "My dad turned up at the cafe yesterday."

He paused after a successful pancake flip. "Your dad? But you've not seen him since you were, what, seven?"

"Something like that," she said. "And not even a Christmas or birthday card since I was eighteen."

"And he just shows up? How did he even know where you are?"

Lee smiled wryly. "The wedding announcement in the gazette."

"Ah. My mother. Sorry!"

"It's okay. Anyway, he was apologetic, but he also had some explanations - and he wants to see me for longer.

Today."

"Wow," he said, carrying plates to the table. "What are you going to do?"

"I think I need to see him. I'm just going to have a million questions otherwise - and as much as I love my mother, and empathise with her not wanting to talk about him... I can't trust her to answer them totally honestly."

"That makes sense. Are you okay seeing him by yourself?"

Lee nodded, disappearing for a minute to retrieve Holly, who was sat as good as gold watching morning cartoons. The promise of pancakes made her less fussy about the telly going off, and she waited until Holly's fingers were picking up sticky pieces of pancake and strawberry before pouring golden syrup across her own.

"I don't want to take madam here though," she said, restarting the conversation as if there hadn't been any interruption. "I'm not introducing her to a man who may well disappear again."

James nodded. "That makes sense - but I've got to work this afternoon..."

"I thought I'd ask Beth, if that's okay with you."

James raised his eyebrows. "He's her dad too, right?"

Lee nodded. "I don't want to tell her just yet, though - you've seen how cut up she is over Caspian. If he just disappears, I don't know how she'll feel. She remembers him even less than I do..."

"If you're sure..."

"I am," Lee said, having a mouthful of pancake and watching Holly make a mess with hers for a moment. "And she'll enjoy spending some time with Holly, and I can suss out what he wants and whether he is actually interested in getting to know us as adults, before Beth needs to know anything."

James didn't look totally convinced, but went back to his pancakes.

"These are delicious," Lee said, putting another couple of slices of strawberry on Holly's high chair table. "You spoil us!"

◆ ◆ ◆

Beth answered her phone on the fifth ring.

"Hey, Lee."

"Beth, how are you doing?"

Beth paused before answering that question; how was she doing? The man she thought she might be falling in love with had left to live on opposite side of this island they called home, and she was worried about her job as the lack of holidaymakers meant a lack of shifts. How truthful should she really be in answer to her sister's question?

"Fine," she answered, lying through her teeth. Her sister had enough stress with her upcoming wedding - she didn't need her sister's love life on her plate too.

"Liar." Well so much for that plan. "Anyway, how does some time with your favourite niece sound? No-one can be miserable around Holly. And I'll even throw in a home-cooked meal."

"By James?"

Lee laughed. "Maybe. Depends what time he gets off work. Please? I have a meeting I could do with going to without a one-year-old!"

Beth sighed. "All right. When do you want me to come over?"

"Is one okay? She'll be down for her nap, so you'll get her cheeriest time afterwards!"

Once she'd put down the phone, Beth looked at herself in the mirror from where she was sat in bed. Her hair was in a messy bun, there were crisp crumbs down her top and she was wearing the same pair of pyjamas that she had thrown on when she'd got home from work Friday night.

"Sort yourself out, Beth Davis," she said. "You are not going to let yourself go to ruin over a man."

Lee tapped her foot as she glanced towards the door five times in the space of a few seconds. They had arranged to meet for a late lunch in Kingsbridge, an old market town with a pretty estuary. She knew if she'd met him in Totnes again it would have set tongues wagging; and Dartmouth was out in case anyone who knew her sister saw her. She did feel a little guilty at lying to Beth, but she reminded herself it was for her sister's own good; there was no good stressing her out over someone who might disappear from their lives just as he had done twenty-odd years ago.

She glanced at her watch, about to feel irritated at him for being late, before realising she was, in fact, early. She was sat opposite to the door in the small cafe half-way up the steep main street, and so when the door opened she instantly saw him.

He leant over and kissed her on the cheek, as if it were the most natural thing in the world - but to Lee it felt a little awkward. "Thank you for meeting me again," he said, as he took a seat.

They ordered sandwiches from the young waitress who had a strong Devonian accent and a pretty smile.

"It's easier when I don't have to go and serve customers between questions," she said with a small smile.

"I want to answer your questions," he said. "And I've got a few questions of my own, if that's okay."

Lee nodded.

"But first - I want to tell you some things. I don't want to speak ill of your mother - I won't speak ill of your mother - but there are some details that she might not have told you. That I want you to know." He took a breath, and a sip of his drink, and continued when Lee didn't comment.

"I married your mum when I was very young - you know that. We were married at twenty, and had you and Beth by the time we were twenty-five."

Lee nodded and drank her tea. This she knew; she vaguely remembered their wedding pictures being on display when she was a young girl. "And then, as you know, I left your mum. I started a relationship with my secretary -

after I'd left your mum, I want to be clear about that. I fell in love… and I realised something."

"What? That you didn't love mum?" She couldn't stop herself butting in.

"No - I still loved your mum. But I realised - or at least, came to terms with, the fact that I'm gay."

She felt her jaw drop. "What?"

"Ah. I only thought recently that your mum had perhaps not told you the entirety of the facts. My secretary… was a man. Is a man. Liam… we married last year."

"I… I…" The waitress came over with their sandwiches, which gave Lee a moment to collect her thoughts. Once she'd checked if they needed any sauces and disappeared back into the kitchen, Lee had finally managed to get the words a little more ordered in her mind.

"I had no idea, dad."

"I was talking to Liam last night, and he suggested - not for the first time - that perhaps you didn't know. And I'd not taken the idea seriously, until we talked yesterday. I feel awful for hurting your mum like I did… but I never cheated on her. And I tried to deny how I felt for a very, very long time."

"But you can't deny who you are," Lee said. "Or who you're meant to be with."

"Exactly."

For a few moments they both ate their sandwiches, and Lee's eyes wandered to the busy street outside. Christmas lights were strung up in windows and across the road in intervals of a couple of metres or so, and many people seemed to be doing their Christmas shopping - although she was fairly sure that a lot of them would travel to the near-ish cities of Plymouth or Exeter to find many of their presents. While the small towns had charm, even she had to admit there were some things you just needed a big city for.

"Why don't you ask your questions," Lee said, "While I let this sink in a bit."

Ted nodded. "I just want to know about your life, really. You went to university in Bristol?"

"No," she said, shaking her head. "London. Studied law. I thought you would have known that..."

He shook his head. "Your mum has not wanted contact with me for a very long time," he said. "And... I didn't try as hard as I should have done to find out."

Lee paused for a moment and took a bite of her sandwich, deciding to move past that comment for now. "I moved back to Bristol, got married, became a partner in a law firm..."

"You were married?"

Lee nodded. "I asked mum to send you an invite..." Her eyebrows knitted together.

"Ah."

"You didn't get it?"

"I would have come, Lee, if I had."

That was a blow that Lee was not expecting. "She never

sent it? She said she wasn't sure about the address…"

"I didn't come here to cause problems between you and your mum," Ted said, wringing his hands and looking a little stressed.

"But she should have sent it. No matter what she felt, how hurt she was, she should have sent you an invitation to my wedding."

Ted nodded, but didn't say anything.

"I feel like a big part of my life has been a complete lie," she said. "Things I always thought were true…"

"I didn't realise you were a partner in a law firm, either, Shirley. That's very impressive."

She smiled briefly. "Thanks. Things are a bit different now, though. My marriage fell apart two years ago, and I moved down here, fell in love with the cafe… I do law work too, on the side, but I needed a change."

"I'm sorry it didn't work out," Ted said, and she felt an honesty to his words that she hadn't expected. There were vague memories in her mind linked to his voice; it was an odd experience, speaking to someone who she hadn't seen in so many years and yet still feeling some link to him, to their past.

"Well, walking in on him with a nurse in our bedroom was pretty much the final nail in the coffin."

"Ah. Yes, I can imagine. But you're getting remarried?"

She smiled more broadly this time. "Yes. To James - the father of my daughter."

"You seem very happy," Ted said, and Lee nodded.

"It was rough, for a while," she admitted. "But I am very happy. It feels like things have finally worked out like they were supposed to."

"I'm really glad to hear that. And what about Elizabeth?"

Lee took a sip of her drink before answering. "She's going through a break up at the minute," she confided, not quite sure why she felt she could trust Ted now with this information. "So I haven't mentioned that you came in the cafe…"

"You don't have to explain," he said.

"But in general, yes, she's doing well. She moved to Dartmouth over the summer, so I get to see her much more. She's working as a tour guide." She slid her phone from her pocket and scrolled through a few images until she found one of her and Beth, taken only a few weeks previously, on the beach in the late autumn sun. Their arms were wrapped around each other and both wore massive grins.

Ted smiled as he looked at the photo, and Lee was pretty sure she saw a tear in his eye.

She put the phone away and was about to ask a question herself, when Ted began to talk.

"I've been such an idiot," he said, his voice sounding a little choked. "I've missed so many years of both of your lives, and I can never get them back. I'm so sorry, Shirley. Lee."

He reached a hand across the table and she let him take hers, feeling tears welling up in her eyes. "It doesn't sound like it was entirely your fault," she said, trying to make him feel a little better. "I can't say I'm not upset - or that I completely understand. But I can see that it's not been easy for you either…"

"Thanks," he said, pulling out a hanky and wiping his eyes. "I honestly didn't plan to get so intense - I just really wanted to see you, and Elizabeth, after all this time."

"I will tell her what you've told me," she promised. "I'm sure she'll have questions too… she doesn't really remember you."

"And I don't think I'll ever forgive myself for that. I've told myself for many years that I was doing the right thing - abiding by your mum's wishes, not bringing the drama of my life into my daughters' lives." He took a deep breath; "But I can see now that I've just been a coward. I should have pushed back - an awfully long time ago."

Lee nodded; she couldn't deny that. "You should have," she said. "But I'm glad you've realised it. And I'm glad you came to find us."

Once they'd said their goodbyes and Lee had watched her father walk back towards his car, she wandered towards the car park overlooking the estuary, but did not return to her own car. Instead, she bought herself an ice cream from a little stand by the water, and found an empty bench. It wasn't hard; being December, holidaymakers were in short supply and the air was fairly bitter. She had been amazed to even find the ice cream stand open; she presumed the Christmas shoppers provided it with some business that made it worth having the young lad stood there all day. She wasn't ready to go home yet, wasn't ready to face Beth. She needed a little time to mull over the information she had been given, and to decide how on earth she would tell her already fragile sister about this. She knew Beth felt she worried too much, but this thing with Caspian had really shaken her sister; she had never seen her so cut up over a man. James had high hopes it would all work out for them, but the realist in Lee - okay, the pessimist - felt like their issues were insurmountable. In fact, she was proud of her normally flaky sister for saying no to moving to Edinburgh with him; she understood the temptation, but with her new life only just set up in Dartmouth, it would have been such a shame to leave it all behind for something so uncertain.

Her mind had wandered from the day's events, and as she focused back on them - and the honeycomb ice cream in her hand - the overwhelming thing she felt was anger. Anger towards her mother - for the lies, for the deception, for not moving on and letting her and Beth have a father in their lives.

Yes, her dad should have pushed harder.

Yes, her mum had been hurt.

But she had been led to believe for a long time that Ted had cheated on her - and run off with another woman; neither of which, it turned out, were true.

And she had always thought he knew what was going on in their lives - and just showed no interest at all.

It seemed that wasn't true either.

She knew she needed to ring her mother, to discuss

everything she had learnt; but she didn't think today was the time for that. She didn't trust herself not to say things she might end up sorely regretting.

Lee took a deep breath before entering the house when she got home, knowing that Beth would easily be able to tell something was up if she weren't very careful. As she entered the house with a smile plastered on her face, she was met by a fair bit of chaos and the sound of Holly giggling. Clothes were strewn on the floor and there were tiny bits of what looked like paper scattered on the floor.

"Hello!" she shouted, and Beth appeared from the kitchen, Holly on her back, a wide grin on her face.

"Hey, Lee! Look, mummy's home!" Holly scrambled off and ran to her mother, who hugged her tightly.

"Sorry, Lee," Beth said, glancing round the hallway. "I meant to tidy up before you got back, but I lost track of time."

Lee laughed. "Don't worry about it. Looks like you've been having lots of fun!"

"We made paper chains to decorate the house with, and then some Christmas confetti for your wedding!" Beth said. "And we got glue all over some clothes…" She bent to pick up the clothes on the floor, and attempted to collect the larger pieces of paper.

"Sounds like you both enjoyed yourself! Leave that, I'll sort it later. Let's put the kettle on, shall we? It's freezing out there."

Beth continued tidying while Lee made hot drinks, and by the time they sat down on the sofa, the house was looking a little closer to its normally tidy state.

"Has she been all right?" Lee asked, sipping her coffee.

"Good as gold," Beth answered. "And you were right - she kept me too busy to wallow, which is definitely a good thing!"

Holly was cuddled up against Lee, and she stroked her hair gently as they spoke. "I don't like to see you wallowing so much, Beth," she said, not for the first time. "How are you doing? Really?"

"I'm okay," Beth said, a little too quickly. "Well," she added, "I'm trying to be. I miss him... and things were going so well, and now it's just over. Gone. Just like that."

"You made the right decision," Lee said, again not for the first time. "You couldn't have moved to Edinburgh, just like that."

Beth nodded, but didn't say anything for a few moments. They drank their drinks in silence, until Beth finally spoke. "I sent him my book," she said. "He's not replied, though."

"I'm sorry. Maybe he's still reading it?"

"Maybe. Or maybe the email address was old... or maybe he just doesn't want to hear from me."

Lee knew that could well be true, and she didn't want to lie; instead she reached over and squeezed Beth's hand. "I'd love to read your book," she said.

Beth mustered up a half-hearted smile. "Thanks. I'm not even sure it's any good."

"Hey, you've written a book - that's more than most of the population can say, isn't it? And I bet it's brilliant."

"Thanks, sis," Beth said, with a more honest grin. "Always my cheerleader."

"Always will be," Lee said, deciding for definite that this was not the right time to burden Beth with the information she had learnt that afternoon. A few more weeks - after Christmas, maybe. Although then she wouldn't be able to invite Ted to her wedding... and she very much wanted to be able to.

She sighed, her mind in muddle, and wished things were a little simpler.

"Wow," James said, at nine o'clock that evening when they were sat on the sofa, Beth having left half an hour previously and Holly happily asleep upstairs. They each had a glass of wine, and Lee's legs were draped across James' lap.

"I know," Lee answered, with a sigh.

"Your mum really kept a lot from you then, huh?"

Lee nodded; "It seems like it. And I'm absolutely furious..."

"I don't blame you."

"I feel like everything I've thought was true about my family has been a lie. Thought dad cheated on mum - not true. Thought he ran off with his female secretary - not exactly true. Thought he wasn't interested in me, or Beth - not bloody true!" She had a large mouthful of wine to punctuate her rant, which allowed James to get a word in.

"And on that topic... do you really not think you should tell her?"

Lee shook her head. "She's cut up about Caspian. I don't want to add to that..."

"She's your sister," James said with a shrug. "I just wouldn't want her to find out some other way, and be angry you've kept it from her."

Lee didn't answer, and James didn't push it; he'd said his bit, and that was enough.

"I'm really angry," Lee finally said, and James ran his fingers up and down her leg.

"I think you have every right to be."

"I'm angry at my mum - for lying, for making out that he was a lot worse than he was, for keeping us from him. But I'm angry at him too - for not fighting a bit harder. I mean, mum says stay away and so he just does? I get for a year or so maybe, but we're talking over twenty years!"

"Are you going to talk to your mum about it?"

Lee nodded; "But it had better be tomorrow. If I do it after a glass of wine, I'll probably say a few things I'll regret." She downed the rest of the wine and balanced the glass precariously on the edge of the sofa's arm. "Just what I need, right before my wedding," she said, getting to her feet. "My absentee father reappearing and a feud with my mother."

James sighed, and grabbed both their glasses to return them to the kitchen, as Lee disappeared to get ready for bed. It seemed like the odds were stacking up against their wedding going without a hitch - despite their reassuring chat the previous day.

Lee took a deep breath and momentarily regretted that it was a mug of coffee in her hand and not something stronger. She reminded herself that she'd made the decision for a good reason; sober Lee was far more likely to give her mother the benefit of the doubt.

James had taken Holly for a walk to the park, although the weather was chilly and the skies grey. She was bundled up in her coat, gloves, hat and scarf and was very excited; Lee just needed some time to talk to her mother alone.

"Shirley, hello," her mother answered. "How are you? And Holly?"

"We're fine thanks mum," Lee said, knowing if she didn't get straight to the point she might chicken out. "I need to talk to you."

"Oh? Is everything all right? Nothing's gone wrong with the wedding, has it? Or between you and James?"

Lee cut across her mother. "It's dad," she said. "He came to see me. And told me - well, everything, I think."

Silence.

"Mum? Did you hear me?"

"Yes."

Lee could feel the anger rising within her. "And you've got nothing to say about that?"

"I didn't know you were in touch with... your father," she eventually said.

"I wasn't. That's the point. I haven't been in touch with him for over twenty years - because of you."

"It was his choice-"

"You told him to stay away."

"He could have-"

"I'm not talking about his failings right now. I'm talking about yours."

"Shirley, there's no need to speak to me like that."

Lee took another deep breath, feeling like she wanted to scream.

"I think there's every need. You stopped me - and Beth - having a father in our lives. I get that he hurt you - more than most people, I get that. But he didn't *actually* cheat on you. He left you. Because he's gay. He's gay, mum, and happily married to a man, and it hurts me you couldn't get over that so we could've had a father in our lives."

She had never in her life spoken so bluntly to her mother, and the force with which the words left her body seemed to take her breath away. Part of her wanted to take it back, to apologise, but she knew she couldn't; she knew she meant it.

She was hurting, and if that meant her mother hurt too… so be it.

When there was no response after an awkwardly long amount of time, Lee spoke again.

"He wants to be in our lives. And I can't see any reason why he shouldn't be."

Silence again - and then a greater silence. Lee pulled the phone away from her ear and confirmed that, yes, her mother had hung up on her.

CHAPTER SEVEN

Five weeks until Christmas

"Hey, Beth," Lee said, wiping down Holly's mouth and the high chair with one hand and holding the phone in the other. "Haven't heard from you in a while! How's things?"

"I spoke to mum," Beth said, and there was a steeliness to her voice that Lee rarely heard - and which set her heart racing. She lifted Holly out of the highchair once she was sure she was clean and had no traces of banana anywhere, and put her down on the living room floor with her toys; she had a feeling this was going to be a long conversation.

"Oh?" She tried to keep her voice light, but was fairly sure she wasn't succeeding.

"Anything you need to tell me?"

So her mother had told Beth. She had never told her not to, she supposed… but she had never thought about the fact that Beth might find out from someone else.

Perhaps James hadn't been completely wrong when he'd said she should tell Beth straight away…

But it was too late for those thoughts now.

"Beth, I—"

"I am absolutely furious with you," Beth said, not letting

her get out the apology she had on her tongue. "How could you? How could you not tell me something as big as this - when I've been to your house? When we've spoken most days? And you meet up with our dad - our dad that we haven't seen since we were little girls - and you don't tell me about it?" Beth's voice got louder as she continued, and Lee winced on the other end of the line.

"I'm sorry," she said. "I really am. Beth, you've got to listen-"

"I don't have to do anything, actually. I thought we were more like friends - thought we told each other things. And then I have to hear from our mother that you're keeping stuff from me? Why? Just tell me that."

"I didn't want to put anything else on your plate," she said. "No, listen, I know it sounds pathetic, but it's the honest truth - you've been through so much lately, with Caspian, and dad turned up out of the blue and dropped all sorts of news on me and... well, I didn't know if he was going to stick around. I was going to tell you, once..."

"Once what? You'd decided I could handle it? I'm a big girl, *Shirley,* I don't need you to decide whether I can hear news or not."

Deserved or not, Lee was hurt by her tone, and she took a few deep breaths before she answered, trying not to get angry or defensive herself. "I wanted to wait until you were doing better. Or until I knew he wanted to stay in our lives. I promise, I just wanted to protect you."

"I'm not a child," Beth said. "And from what mum said to me, in a very angry and bitter conversation I'll have you know, is that he does want to be in our lives. Maybe you just wanted him to yourself?"

"No, Beth, I promise, it's not like that - please, come over, we can talk. There's so much I need to tell you."

"It's a bit late for that," Beth said, and for a moment there was silence on the other end of the line. "I can't talk to you right now Lee. Bye."

Once again, Lee found herself hung up on, and she felt a little in shock. She couldn't remember the last time Beth had spoken to her like that - probably not since they were teenagers. And she had to make herself ask the most difficult question - was Beth right? And James right? Should she have told her sister straight away?

She fumbled around to find the remote, and flicked through the channels until she found some cartoons. Holly seemed more than happy with that development; Lee curled up on the sofa and pressed her face into the pillow for a few moments, letting her tears fall without Holly seeing them.

What a mess.

Her mother wasn't speaking to her.

Her sister wasn't speaking to her.

She was getting married in a month, and hosting Christmas for their combined families days later.

How on earth was she going to make everything right again?

There was something truly spectacular about Edinburgh as it prepared for Christmas, Caspian Blackwell thought as he rode the bus into town at a ridiculously early hour of the morning. The sky was still dark and, as they passed Haymarket and made their way into the city centre, he found himself craning his neck to see the lights of the shops and the hotels all the way down Princes Street. That was one bonus of having early meetings with members of his team - he got to see the lights before the town got busy with Christmas shoppers. And busy it got; despite the cold weather, despite the fact that it seemed to rain an awful lot, despite the fact that he could swear it was dark by three in the afternoon most days - people flocked to the town centre. The festive season only brought more of them, and he couldn't blame them; there was something magical about the lights. He had made a trip the previous weekend to The Dome, which was the most festive place he thought he'd ever been; the pillars outside were wrapped in lights and ribbon, and inside the bar was the most enormous and beautiful Christmas tree he had ever seen. The whole place smelt of Christmas - nutmeg and cinnamon, cloves and pine, and he had spent a good hour by the bar, nursing a whiskey and wishing Beth was there with him. Thinking about how her eyes would have lit up as she surveyed the Christmas decorations, or the novel she might have been inspired to write just by being there.

He shook his head; he'd told himself he would not think about Beth Davis. Not sat in that bar, and not now on the bus. It had been weeks since he'd left Dartmouth, moved everything he had 600 miles and left the woman he…

The woman he couldn't stop thinking about.

He'd asked her to come to Edinburgh; and she'd said no.

Part of him understood that, of course it did; it was a crazy request. He had felt crazy asking it, but he'd hoped that somehow, part of her would have been crazy enough to say yes. After all, this was a girl he'd met swimming in the ocean late at night in her underwear. This was a girl who'd fallen in love with a town and a flat above a chip shop and relocated to start over...

But she'd said no. And he had felt the pain of that rejection keenly every day since - no matter how many times he told himself to not think about Elizabeth Davis. It didn't help, of course, that he still ended up talking about her. After she'd sent him that manuscript to read, he'd felt compelled to pass it on to someone who knew a lot more than he did about such things. Caspian had really enjoyed it, but he was willing to accept that he might be slightly biased when it came to anything to do with the petite blonde woman who had made him act more spontaneously than he had in many years. But when a friend in the industry liked it too - liked it so much he wanted to discuss getting it published - well, he'd had no choice but to talk about her. And to write to her...

It had been a while since there had been any real contact, and deep down he thought that was probably for the best. That way this pain in his chest would disappear, eventually. Right? The sense that something was missing whenever he saw anything new or did anything exciting... that had to fade. Eventually.

He nearly missed his stop, and got to the door just as the bus driver closed it. The driver sighed as it reopened, and Caspian apologised, stepping onto the quiet Edinburgh street and meandering towards the office. How the company had ever got offices in the centre of Edinburgh, he would never know, but they certainly made work a bit more enjoyable.

As he stepped through the glass double doors, he wondered if things would ever be as enjoyable as the weeks he had spent dating Elizabeth Davis.

CHAPTER EIGHT

Four weeks until Christmas

"I can't go," Lee said, sat on the bed and staring into the mirror on their built-in wardrobe. "I can't. Not with things the way they are."

"Lee," James said, sitting on the bed next to her and putting and arm around her shoulder. She leant against him, allowing her head to drop onto his shoulder, feeling some comfort from his strong, steady presence - but not enough to make her go. "It's your hen party. You can't not go."

"My sister hates me. My mother hates me. How can I go to a hen party with them when we've not sorted this whole mess out?"

"Maybe this will be what sorts it out," James said. "Maybe they'll put it aside for your hen party and you can move past it."

Lee snorted. "Have you met my mother? There is absolutely no way this is going to disappear because I'm getting married. Anyway, I bet half of them think it's ridiculous me having a hen party, when it's my second time down the aisle."

There was a pause then; Lee hadn't really meant to say that. They were concerns she had only shared with Beth

- not with James. She hadn't wanted to burden him… but then that had also got her into trouble recently.

"Is that how you feel?" he asked quietly, not quite meeting her eye in the mirror. She could feel his curly hair against her cheek and she closed her eyes in case she saw hurt in his.

"No," she said quickly, and then decided the truth was better. "Maybe."

He pulled his arm away and turned to face her, and she forced herself to look him in the eye and face the hurt that was pooling there.

"Lee, I've said before, if you don't want to get married, I don't want you to feel forced into it." His voice caught slightly in his throat.

"I do want to marry you," Lee whispered. "I just have these worries…"

"Tell me," he said. "Let me help."

"You can't."

"Tell me anyway."

"I don't want to hurt you."

"Tell me anyway."

Lee took a deep breath; keeping things secret hadn't been doing her any good lately. "I'm worried… about what people will think. I worry they think I shouldn't have a big wedding, or a white dress, or a hen party, because I've done all this before. I worry…" She took another deep breath, and forced herself to carry on. "I worry that they'll be thinking that this won't last, because my last marriage didn't."

"Do you think it'll last?" James asked.

Lee didn't hesitate. "Yes."

"Then I don't care if anybody's thinking that - which, by the way, I don't think they are. I am not going to cheat on you. You are not going to leave me at the alter. Right?"

Lee gave a weak smile. "Right."

"But you are going to go to this hen party."

Lee groaned.

"Lee, you'll regret it if you don't. Beth has planned it for you - yes, she might be angry at you right now, but she's also your sister, and she also loves you. So get dressed - anyway, Holly and I have big plans for a movie and ice cream, and you're not invited."

Lee laughed, and took his hand as she pulled herself up off the bed. "Holly's bedtime is in an hour," she reminded him.

"What you don't know won't hurt you," he said with a grin, pressing a kiss to her lips. "You deserve a hen party, and a big wedding, and you're going to have it all."

"I love you," she said.

"I love you too."

When he'd left the room, she rifled through her wardrobe, trying to find the fitted black dress that always made her feel better - mum tum or not. Once she'd located it near the back of her wardrobe - it had been quite a long time since she'd dressed up and gone out - she sat back down on the bed and pulled out her phone. She was going to ring, but chickened out, deciding instead a text would have to do.

Is tonight still happening? XX She typed, and let her finger hover over send for a full minute before hitting it.

The response was mercifully quick, and Lee held her breath while reading it: *Of course it is. We'll talk properly tomorrow - I want you to enjoy tonight. X*

The kiss at the end buoyed her spirits, and Lee began to get ready, feeling a little less apprehensive about the evening ahead.

James dropped her off at the hotel where she was due to have afternoon tea with the closest ladies in her life. Holly napped happily in the back of the car, and Lee didn't bother to comment on the fact that she was not going to sleep properly that night; James knew that already, and he knew Lee would be out until fairly late. She knew he could handle it - and one night of bad sleep wasn't going to do her much harm.

"You look fantastic," James said, giving her a kiss and leaning across her to open the passenger door, encouraging her out. "I'll see you later. Stay out as late as you like."

She grinned; "What if I'm home in an hour's time?"

"Then I'll drive you back out again." He glanced in the back to make sure Holly was asleep. "No strippers though, hey?"

Lee laughed. "I told Beth to make sure it was a tame

evening, don't worry - after all, both our mothers will be there!"

She pressed a kiss to James' lips before getting out the car and making sure her little black dress was pulled straight. She opened the back door and pressed a gentle kiss on Holly's forehead, stroking a curl away from her eyes and smiling. "Love you both."

Feeling a little nervous still, she walked across the gravelled drive way to the grand front door. Afternoon tea, followed by cocktails and a few games - that's what Beth had said was the plan for the evening. She just hoped all the guests would be speaking to her...

Alcohol was abundant at the afternoon tea, which Lee was grateful for. A constantly full glass of champagne made it easier to forget the fact that her mother was sat two metres away, not speaking to her. Beth had given her a hug, and a smile that made Lee feel everything would be okay in the end. Everyone else, of course, was unaware of the tensions between the three Davis women, and so Lee tried to throw herself into their excitement for her wedding.

"This is delicious," Sadie, James's mother, said, with a broad smile and a friendly squeeze to Lee's arm. "I haven't had an afternoon tea in years - such a good idea."

Lee nodded her head to Beth. "All Beth's doing," she said. "Although you're right, it is delicious!"

"So," James's sister Therese asked, "Is everything ready for the wedding?"

"I think so!" Lee said as she finished a mouthful of scone. "I hope so at least. Dresses and suits are bought, flowers are organised, numbers confirmed... let's hope nothing's been forgotten!"

"Although I do think you're a little crazy, offering to host Christmas for everyone days after your wedding!" Therese's wife Tamsin added.

"Ah," Lee said with a laugh. "Well, that one was James's idea - although to be fair, he does all of the cooking! And I wasn't going to disrupt a family tradition."

Beth topped up her glass with champagne. "How many is it you've got coming?" she asked, and Lee felt a warming inside her at Beth joining in the conversation.

"Um..." Lee began to count in her head, feeling slightly panicked as she did so. "Twelve, I think!"

Gina let out a low whistle. "Crazy woman!" she said with a grin.

"Now, that's enough about Christmas," Beth said. "As you all know, we are here to celebrate Lee's last days as *Shirley* Davis, before she marries the sexiest police officer around-" there were laughs and groans from his family members - "And becomes Mrs Shirley Knight."

"Less of the Shirley, sis," Lee said. "There might've been some people who didn't realise that was my full name!" She saw her mother's face tighten, and regretted her champagne-fuelled words. It seemed like Sadie was picking up on the tensions; that or she had impeccable timing.

"It's a beautiful name," she said, "And I'm lucky to be

getting a beautiful daughter-in-law who's given me a beautiful granddaughter!"

There was a collective 'awww' before Beth moved them all along.

"Time to play a game," she said, handing out pieces of paper and pens in a much more organised fashion than Lee would've expected. "Who knows the bride best? No cheating - and as quiz master my ruling is final!"

There had been some friendly competition within the game, which had seen Gina win with the most knowledge about Lee - something which did not help the atmosphere between her and her mother. As everyone tucked in to yet more sweet treats, Lee moved round to sit next to her mother on a green chintz sofa.

"Hi, mum," she said, very conscious of the fact that her mother had not yet spoken to her.

"Shirley," she said, sipping her tea and averting her eyes from her daughter's.

"I'm sorry for how we left our last conversation," Lee forced herself to say. It was at least bordering on the truth; she *was* upset about how their phone call had ended. She didn't feel what she'd said had been wrong - but perhaps the way she had said it could have been toned down.

"I don't want to discuss this here," Tina said, barely moving her lips. Lee noticed Beth looking over in concern, and hoped she wouldn't try to join them; she could only cope with one at a time today. Besides, if the three of them were huddled together looking serious, it would be rather hard to avoid questions.

"Me neither, mum," Lee said truthfully. "But I would like us to be able to be civil with each other - even if we haven't sorted through everything."

There was a moment's pause, then a curt nod; Lee accepted that was the best she was likely to get. She gave her mother's hand a squeeze, and then moved away to mingle with her guests.

*

◆ ◆ ◆

As the clock approached half eleven, only Lee, Beth and Gina remained in the cocktail bar, which Lee had been pleased had remained stripper-free. Cocktails were flowing a little too freely, and Lee was pretty sure both Gina's and Beth's voices were slurred - and possibly her own, too. At some point in the evening, Beth had managed to wrestle L plates and a tacky looking veil onto Lee, and so it couldn't be more obvious that she was a woman in her last throes of freedom - well, as free as an engaged woman with a one-year-old was every likely to be.

"I'm sorry," Lee said, when Gina had gone to the toilets and she was left with her sister and a large pitcher of strawberry daiquiris. " I'm so- so sorry. I was wrong, I wanted to protect you, but you're not a baby. I know that. I just worry about you."

Beth leant to put a hand on Lee's knee, but accidentally overshot and landed half in her lap. They both giggled, and as Beth righted herself she said, "I know. I know. I overreacted."

"You didn't. I'm sorry. Sorry from the bottom of my heart."

"What are you sorry about?" Gina - who had obviously stopped off at the bar on her way back from the bathroom - asked. "Sounds serious."

"She didn't tell me our dad's back. And he's gay."

"He's gay?" Gina said, jaw dropping. "The guy who came in the café the other day?"

Lee nodded. "Gay, married to his secretary - male secretary, obviously."

"Wow. And you said your life was boring!" Gina said with a laugh. "Gay father, family secret, run off from your cheating ex to buy a café in a small town in Devon... Need I go on?"

"I don't think so," Lee said with a giggle. "Definitely does not sound boring!"

When she woke up the next day, Lee had a banging headache and only a hazy memory of getting home that evening. She was in her own bed, in her pyjamas, but she was pretty sure James would have been to thank for that; she was convinced she would have gone to bed in her dress and heels if she'd been making the decisions. She could feel from how dry her skin was that she was still wearing make-up, and when she turned her head she was very grateful to see a large glass of water on the bedside table, which she gulped eagerly.

"Mama!" she heard from down the hall, and in spite of her delicate state she couldn't help but smile at the sound.

"Shh, we're going to let mama sleep. Come on, we'll have pancakes for breakfast!"

"Mama!"

"Shhh."

"Bet?" The sound at the end of Beth's name hadn't quite made it, but Lee was pretty sure that was what her daughter was saying, even through the closed door.

"Auntie Beth is sleeping too. Come on, pancake time!"

The noise died down, and Lee tried to remember getting home... there was a fuzzy memory of a taxi ride with Beth, and she presumed Beth had decided to stay here instead of heading back to Dartmouth in another taxi.

Once she'd drunk most of the water, thrown on a dressing gown to ward against the chill that had set in, and removed the panda-esque traces of make-up on her face, Lee headed downstairs and was greeted with a big grin from her daughter, strapped in her highchair and making an incredible mess with pancakes and strawberries.

"Mama!"

"Morning my Holly berry," she said, planting a kiss on her head before turning in search of coffee. James was a step ahead of her it, seemed, and handed her a steaming mug.

"You're too good to me," she said, pressing a kiss to his

cheek with a smile.

"Good night?"

"I think so," she said with a slightly sheepish grin. "Beth is talking to me, anyway."

"Well, since she's in our spare room, I hope she is! And your mum?"

"Eh," Lee said, sipping the coffee and wincing slightly as it burnt her tongue. "She left before the cocktails, but she did say goodbye…"

"Sounds like progress."

"I need to talk to her properly…" She ran a hand through her hair and stifled a yawn. "But not today!"

"You need some food - once that coffee's got into your system!" he said, pulling eggs from the fridge. "Fried or scrambled?"

"Far too good to me. Scrambled, please - and do you mind doing some for Beth? She always has to eat after drinking."

Beth appeared just as James was serving up, looking as tired as Lee felt, and smiled as she saw the breakfast being put on the table.

"I could get used to this," she said. She was wearing a pair of Lee's pyjamas, which she presumed James had sourced for her - Lee certainly couldn't remember digging them out. "I need to stop drinking," she said, scarfing down the eggs and thanking James for the mug of tea he brought over.

"It was a hen do!" James said. "I think you're allowed to

let your hair down."

"Hmmm," Beth said, and Lee wondered if there was a little more to that statement than she was letting on - but that wasn't something Lee was about to explore with a hangover.

"I haven't drunk that much in... well, a couple of years if I'm honest. Before we had this little one, that's for sure," Lee said, ruffling Holly's hair.

"Gina's a bad influence," Beth said, and they both laughed, knowing full well that they'd all egged each other on.

"I'd better text her," Lee said. "Make sure she got home okay."

"If I remember rightly, she was in a better state than us," Beth said. "So I don't think you need to worry too much! If we managed to get home, I'm sure she did."

Lee nodded, but fired off a quick message anyway. She was relieved to receive a thumbs up back almost instantly, and didn't press for any more.

"Thanks for yesterday, Beth," Lee said, crunching on some extra toast James had brought over. "I really enjoyed myself."

Beth grinned. "You're welcome." She glanced at James; "And the s-t-r-i-p-p-e-r wasn't too bad, was he?"

Lee laughed at the look of shock on James's face, and even Beth couldn't keep up the pretense for more than a couple of seconds.

"Tell me what he said then," Beth asked, curled up on the sofa with her third mug of tea. "What does he look like? What's he like?"

James and Holly were upstairs playing, and Lee was finally able to have the heart to heart with her sister that she'd needed to have for days.

"He's older - of course. Grey hair, beard, skinny, quite distinguished looking really," Lee said, sipping her coffee. She needed the caffeine if she was going to make it through the day - and the night, as James had to work and Holly would undoubtedly not sleep well after the change in her routine. "And he said... so much, Beth. And he'll want to say it all to you, too, I'm sure - answer your questions. I keep thinking of questions I should have asked..."

"So what mum always told us..."

"Lies, mainly, from what I can gather," Lee said, trying not to let anger seep into her voice but struggling. "I haven't really spoken to her - well, she hasn't really spoken to me about it. But she hasn't denied it."

"To think," Beth said, glancing out of the window at the dark clouds rolling in. "All those years we could have had a dad in our lives. All those years where we've been thinking he was completely in the wrong."

"Don't," Lee said, putting her mug down on the coffee table with a little more force than was really required. "I can't think about it without getting angry."

"So where does he live?"

"London. Has done for years, apparently. All that time I

was in university there…" She sighed.

"I want to meet him. Again, I mean," Beth said.

"What if we went to London? I was thinking, I'd like to see his life, maybe meet his husband…"

Beth nodded. "I can easily get the time off from work - but what about you? You've got Holly, the cafe, the law work - not to mention a wedding in less than a month and a million people coming over for Christmas!"

Lee groaned. "Don't remind me! But this is important too. What if we went whenever James is next off? Take the train, leave early, come back late. James can look after Holly. We could do a bit of Christmas shopping too…"

Beth smiled. "Sounds good. Anything to fill my weekends, to be honest…"

Lee squeezed her hand. "I'm sorry it's so tough."

Beth sighed; "Hearing from him, hearing he liked my book… that was so wonderful. But now the pain's almost worse again… like it's opened up a wound that was starting to heal. And I just want to ring him…"

"You could," Lee said.

"But what would I say? Nothing's changed. He left, not wanting to do long distance. I'm not going to move to Edinburgh - certainly not for the foreseeable future." She sighed. "It sucks - I meet a guy who seems perfect, and life has to get in the way."

"I know," Lee said. "And I'm sorry if I've made things harder for you than they should have been."

Beth shook her head. "I get why you kept it from me... but you shouldn't have done. I'm not a baby, and I don't need protecting from the world."

"I know." There was a pause as they heard a bang upstairs and Lee listened out for any tears, but it sounded like they were playing just as happily as before. "That's amazing news about your book though - that a publisher likes it!"

"It's terrifying," Beth admitted, running her finger around the top of her mug. "And amazing. I feel like I should be angry with Cas for passing it on without asking me, but I just can't be - and I can't believe someone's interested in publishing it!"

"I can - you've always been creative. You just needed to find the right outlet." Lee grinned. "Now can I read it?"

Beth nodded; "Be nice though!"

"When am I ever not?"

As they stood on the platform at Totnes train station, Lee felt both excitement and nerves. She hadn't been on a train in a long time, and the thought of spending the day with her sister in London made her feel like she was younger and more free again. As they would be doing the journey in a single day, they had decided to take the train - neither fancied doing that amount of driving in one go - and it also meant they could enjoy some Christmassy drinks in the capital.

It was ridiculously early, but there were still a few people milling about at the two-platformed station. The signs always made Lee laugh whenever she saw them; one simply labelled 'The North'. That was, of course, pretty much everywhere; only Plymouth and Cornwall were the other direction. The men and women in suits on the platform were, she presumed, commuting to work. The sky was still pitch black, and Beth appeared with only a few minutes to spare, carrying a takeaway mug of tea in her hand.

"I thought you were going to miss it!" Lee said, sipping from her own mug of coffee and checking the board again.

"You worry too much," Beth said with a grin. "I bet you were here twenty minutes early!"

Lee laughed. "Something like that."

"To be honest, I wasn't expecting it to be so hard to park - what are people doing here so early!"

"Going to work, I guess!" Lee said as the train pulled in.

They chatted and read as the train chugged through both of their former home cities on the way to London. Lee was reading Beth's novel, and Beth found herself feeling so nervous about her feedback that she had to read herself in order to distract herself. She sank into a comfortable old Poirot book that she'd bought from a second hand bookshop in Dartmouth, and for a good hour neither of them spoke.

As Beth's stomach began to rumble, Lee put her Kindle down and rooted around in her bag, pulling out two muffins and two bananas.

Beth laughed, but gratefully took them. "Always organised!"

"Comes from having a toddler."

"Nah," Beth said with a grin. "You've always been like this!"

"This book is brilliant," Lee said, biting into a muffin. "Honestly, Beth, I'm so impressed - I keep forgetting that you wrote it and just getting lost in it. It's incredible - no wonder someone's interested in publishing it."

Beth blushed. "You really think so? I think I need some more impartial people to read it, give me some honest criticism. Or mum, maybe..."

They both laughed; their mother was certainly blunt, and never held back if she felt criticism was due.

"I know I'm your sister," Lee said, "But I honestly think it's incredible. I'm so proud of you!"

When their train pulled in, they both hurried to get off, knowing that they didn't have long to reacquaint themselves with the tube and get to Covent Garden in time for their lunch with their dad. Lee had lived in London while at university, and so was fairly confident at getting around - although it had been some years - so Beth let her take the lead, and trusted her to get them there.

In truth, she was nervous; she could barely remember her father, and hadn't spoken to him in many, many years. Crazy thoughts were going through her head; what if he didn't like her? What if she wasn't what he was expecting? What if, compared to Lee - who was a lawyer, owned a business, had a child, was getting married - he was disappointed?

They re-emerged from the tube into the weak winter sunlight, and Lee glanced at her watch. "Ten minutes," she said. "Perfect - although I'm going to have to search for directions to the restaurant, not somewhere I've been before."

◆ ◆ ◆

"There he is," Lee whispered, pointing to Ted sat at a table for three in the corner of the modern-looking restaurant. His grey hair was neatly combed, and he wore a brown leather jacket over a shirt. He seemed to be perusing the menu.

"You know I barely remember what he looked like," Beth said. "It's not like mum had any photos up around the house."

He looked up then and stood, raising a hand to wave. Lee smiled, and together they weaved through the busy tables to reach him.

"Shirley - sorry, Lee," he said, leaning over to hug her. "It's great to see you again. And Elizabeth…"

There was a slightly more awkward hug, before they all took a seat - but Ted couldn't tear his eyes off his youngest daughter for several minutes.

"Can I take your order?" A friendly, if over-enthusiastic, waiter came over, and they quickly ordered drinks, needing a little time to actually look at the menu before ordering lunch.

"People generally call me Beth," she said, as a silence threatened to take hold.

"Beth," he said. "I'm so pleased to see you. I know it's been far too long. I'm guessing Lee has filled you in on what I told her?"

She nodded, feeling suddenly shy - not a trait she regularly displayed.

"Well," he said, picking up the menu. "It means a lot to me, that you both came."

Once they'd ordered, they chatted about Lee's upcoming wedding, and Lee showed him some more recent pictures of Holly, which he said all the right things to.

"I'd like you to come," Lee blurted out over dessert, causing all three of them to pause with spoons in mid-air. "To my wedding," she said. "You... and your husband."

Ted smiled. "That would be wonderful. But your mother..."

"Will cope," Lee cut across him. "I won't lie, things are a bit frosty between us at the minute. But it's my wedding day, and I'd like you to be there."

"Then I'd be honoured," Ted said. "I'll have to dust off my suit!"

They finished their desserts and, after a long period of not joining in the conversation, Beth was slightly startled to be addressed.

"Lee told me you work at Agatha Christie's place, is that

right?" Ted asked.

Beth nodded; "For now," she said. "I don't know how long they'll have shifts for me."

Lee nudged her. "Don't play it down! Tell him what else you've been doing."

Beth felt about twelve again, being pushed by her sister to say the right thing. She didn't know why she was feeling so reticent; it certainly wasn't her usual attitude.

"I've written a novel," she said. "A mystery novel - and there's a publisher interested in it."

Ted put down his glass and smiled. "That's incredible!" he said. "What an achievement. Is it Christie-inspired?"

Beth felt a little more like she could open up, and so she chatted for a while about her novel, which bits were inspired by her job and what her next plans were - which, frankly, she wasn't sure about. She supposed she would try to write another novel - although the first had seemed to just come to her. What if nothing else was forthcoming?

They wandered along the river after lunch, wrapped up in coats and scarves but enjoying the sunshine that had broken through. Christmas was definitely in the air, and when Ted suggested having hot chocolate from a stand overlooking a huge Christmas tree with an ice rink around it, the girls couldn't refuse.

"I just want to say," he said, as they leant against a wall and watched the skaters. "Again, to both of you, just how sorry I am. I know I can never make up for the many, many years we've lost - but I really hope we can start again. I know you're adults, and you've got your own lives - but I'd really like to be part of them. In whatever way you would like me to."

Lee glanced at Beth, and for a moment neither spoke, taking in his words and letting their own feelings about this bizarre situation swirl around.

"I think we'd like that too… dad," Beth said."

With only a few hours before their train would leave, once they'd said goodbye to Ted, Beth and Lee hurried back to the underground and headed for Oxford Street. When they were younger, their mum had taken them there to see the Christmas lights most years, and they would often visit a department store Father Christmas. They were fond memories, and both wanted to relive them, for a moment - as well as indulge in a little pre-Christmas retail therapy.

The sky had begun to darken, and so by the time they reached Oxford Street the lights were on in all their glory. Giant bows made of lights were strung at intervals down the street, and at one end it look like lights were raining from the sky. Silver stars hung as if suspended by magic, and for several minutes the two stood, jaws slightly open, taking in the magic of the scenery.

"I love Christmas," Lee said with a relaxed sigh.

"I know you do!" said Beth.

"I know a Christmas wedding seems crazy and stressful," Lee said. "But there is some magic about this time of year, isn't there…"

Beth glanced at the lights once more, and then at the busy shoppers darting in and out of the well-lit shops. "I guess," she said. "More so if you've got someone to share it with, I think."

Lee linked arms with Beth and gave her a squeeze. "You've got me. You've got all of us - and there's someone out there who is absolutely perfect for you, Beth, I'm sure of it. By next Christmas, you'll be feeling the magic with someone too."

Beth sighed, and dragged her sister off to the nearest shop. She was secretly very concerned that she had found the person who was absolutely perfect for her - but that the world had conspired against things working out.

It was dark out - as it seemed to be most of the time - and Caspian sat drinking a bottle of beer and watching the world go by from his flat window. Like many Edinburgh flats it was an old building, with high ceilings, large bay windows and at least one resident mouse. He missed his house in Strete, which he hadn't yet got round to renting out. It made no sense to leave it empty; when he went back to the area he could always stay with his mum, and with the amount of work he had to do at the minute, he wouldn't have much time to travel. That wasn't even considering the sheer distance between Edinburgh and the South West of England.

And yet... renting it out felt like he was turning his back on a place and a part of his life he'd really enjoyed. Travelling for work but being based in Devon, seeing his mum nearly every Sunday…

Beth. As usual she permeated his thoughts, and he tried very hard to not picture her grinning at him, having just teased him about something predictable he had done.

His phone lit up on the table, and he was embarrassed that he instantly hoped it would be Beth. But then why would it? They hadn't said they would stay in touch; he hadn't called her. Not even about her book…

He glanced at the screen and smiled; *Mum.* Pretty much the only non-work-related call he ever got.

"Hi, mum."

"Hello, Caspian dear. Is this a good time?"

"Always a good time to talk to you," he said, putting his feet up on a chair and taking another swig of beer. "How are you doing?"

"Such a charmer," she said with a laugh. She proceeded to fill him in on her day to day life; a WI meeting, Christmas presents she'd been buying and wrapping, and his plans for Christmas.

"You know I'll be spending it with you," he said. "I'm just not sure when I'll make it down."

"You sound sad," Mandy said, and Caspian briefly considered lying, before thinking better of it. His mother aways knew when he wasn't telling the truth - it was a skill she had honed from when he was a little boy.

"I am," he said. "But I'm trying not to be."

"I hate to hear you down," she said. "You seemed so

happy…"

"I was." That thought made him even more miserable, and he took a longer swig of his beer.

"Do I need to have words with Beth for breaking your heart?"

Caspian gave a short, sharp laugh. "I told you mum - it wasn't like that. She couldn't move here. I couldn't do long distance. No heart breaking."

"Hmm," she said. "I'm not sure I believe that. But I'm glad I don't have to read her the riot act - I liked her."

"Me too," Caspian said. "I- I thought she might have been, you know. The one. It sounds stupid…"

"It doesn't."

"She's the only person - you excluded, of course - that I've ever felt I could be completely myself around. But who also made me act like a completely different person. I know that makes no sense… But I liked the person I was with her." He sighed, surprised at himself for opening up so much; perhaps it was the beer, or the distance, or the fact he couldn't see his mother's face.

Perhaps he was simply lonely.

"I miss her. And I miss you," he said.

"I miss you too, son. But it will all work out. It always does, in the end. And if it hasn't worked out-"

"It's not the end," he finished, having heard the saying many times over the years. "I'll try to employ your optimism!"

"I'm always right!" She said with a laugh. "You sound like you're working too hard, too - that can't be helping things. Can you not wrap up a bit early and come home for a couple of weeks for Christmas? You can work from home - you've done that plenty of times before."

Caspian ran his fingers absent-mindedly over the stubble he had let grow across his chin. "Maybe. Let me see what I can do."

"It's been a long time since I've gone this long without seeing you," she reminded him, making him feel guilty.

"I'll try - I promise."

CHAPTER NINE

Three weeks until Christmas

After three lullabies, a story and a second drink of milk, Lee had finally got Holly fast asleep in her cot. She and James tended to take turns getting her down - except for nights like tonight, when he was working a night shift and the parenting was left to her alone. She flicked the kettle on and stifled a yawn, wondering how early was acceptable to get into bed. When James was working, she tended to have an earlier night, catching up on the sleep that she often missed. She had plenty of law work to get on with the next day, including helping a father work through the paperwork for a custody battle in a rather acrimonious divorce, which made her a little miserable right before Christmas. Some extra sleep definitely wouldn't go amiss.

As she waited for the kettle to boil and her tea to brew, she scrolled through the two to-do lists on her phone - one for the wedding, and one for Christmas. Luckily, most of the Christmas preparation was being sorted by James, so she just had a few presents to finalise, and some last minute wedding confirmations. Almost everything was ready, and she was trying to let herself feel excited about the wedding. The idea of being married to James made her smile whenever she thought of it; the idea of walking down the aisle and saying vows that promised she would stay with James for the rest of her life - and so that was what she focussed on. That was what she got excited about - and after seeing how excited everyone had been at her hen party, some of her previous worries had faded a little.

She had just settled down with a steaming mug of tea and the television remote, with the curtains drawn and a fire lit in the fireplace, when she heard a knock at the door. It was not something she was used to - their driveway was hard enough to find when people were actually looking for it, so unexpected visitors weren't common. She paused for a second to check no noise was coming through the baby monitor, then headed to the front door to find out who it could be.

"Hi, Shirley." Her mother stood with a thick black coat and scarf wrapped around her, her face set and her hair blowing a little in the evening wind. The mist was setting in around them, and it gave the whole evening a rather eerie look.

"Mum," Lee said, standing to one side to let her through the doorway. "Come in, it's freezing."

"Thanks." She wiped her feet on the mat before removing her black boots, and she did not speak as she hung her coat and scarf on the rack beside the door.

"It's warmer in the living room," Lee said, wondering how to politely ask what on earth she was doing here.

Still barely a word had been said, and when Tina sat herself down on the sofa, Lee remained standing.

"Tea?" she asked finally, and when Tina nodded she was grateful to have an excuse to escape the room for a minute.

Her mother rarely turned up out of the blue - and to do so without saying why she was there instantly was unheard of. There was also the fact that she hadn't spoken to her mother since the hen do, and not properly then - things needed to be discussed, but it always seemed to be a task Lee pushed to the bottom of her to-do list.

The kettle seemed to boil ridiculously quickly, and before she knew it the tea was ready and she had no reason not to face her mother in the other room.

"James not here?" Tina asked as she took the mug of tea from her daughter.

"Working tonight,"   Lee said. "He won't be back 'til the early hours of the morning."

"That must be tough."

"It's not too bad," Lee said. "He does a lot with Holly the rest of the time, so the odd night I have to do on my own every couple of weeks isn't too bad. They've cut back on his night shifts since we had her, which is great."

"You're lucky," Tina said.

"I know." Lee paused, and decided to dive straight in. It would be midnight at this rate by the time they got on to the reason Tina had driven two hours, late at night to visit unannounced. "Is... is everything okay, mum?"

Tina took a sip of her tea, and for a moment Lee didn't think she was going to answer. "No. We need to talk."

Lee nodded.

"I don't like arguing with you, Shirley, and I didn't like the way you spoke to me on the phone the other day. No, let me finish." Seeing Lee was about to interrupt, she put her hand up to halt her, and Lee felt a little like a naughty child. "But you were right. And I was wrong."

They were words she didn't think she had ever heard from her mother before, and it took a few moments for them to sink in.

"Over the years," Tina said, staring into the fire as the flames danced and licked the wood and coal. "Over the years I have told myself many reasons why I hadn't been completely honest with you - both of you- about your father." Lee thought she saw tears in her mother's eyes, but said nothing; she knew this was not a time to interrupt. "I was, understandably I think, hurt when he left me. Hurt by him ending our marriage. Hurt to find out that... well, that he had no interest in me. I asked him - I told him - to stay away. I was too hurt to see him." She took a deep breath. "And then, over the years... I didn't want you to be teased at school because your father was with another man. I didn't want him to be in our lives, to have to see him happy knowing... knowing how broken my heart was." She gulped; "How broken my heart is. Shirley, I don't like to talk of these things, but I want you to understand why I did what I did."

Lee nodded; "I understand you were hurt, mum. I don't know how I'd feel if Nathan had to be part of my life..."

"Over the years, it got easier. He pushed less. I'm not blaming him..."

"He has a decent share of the blame too, mum - I'm well aware of that."

Tina nodded, and Lee was proud of herself for how calm she was remaining.

"But… I asked you to send him an invite to my wedding. I thought you had. But now I wonder if it never got sent."

"That…" Tina's voice cracked, and she fished around in her handbag to find a handkerchief. She dabbed at her eyes and took a steadying breath. "That was unforgivable. I can only apologise. I don't think I can even explain why I did it, but it was wrong of me."

Lee nodded again, and for the first time that evening, Tina looked her daughter straight in the eye.

"I know you and Elizabeth don't tell me everything, but all I ever want is for you both to be happy. I am so proud of you, Shirley, and I cannot bear to think I have destroyed our relationship."

Tears were running down Tina's face, carrying her eye make-up with them, and Lee found herself sniffing too.

"It's not destroyed, mum. I won't lie, it's going to take me a long time to get over. But it doesn't change the fact that you're my mum, and I know how much hard work you put in to raising Beth and me."

She leant forward on the sofa and gave her mum a hug, and felt a huge sense of relief when it was reciprocated. No, everything could not be sorted in one night - but perhaps now they could begin to move on.

When she pulled away and reached in her pocket for a tissue, Lee regarded her usually unflappable mother and felt one more thing needed to be said. "I want him at this wedding, mum."

Tina took a deep, steadying breath. "I thought you

would."

"You'll be okay, seeing him there?"

Tina nodded, although it wasn't entirely convincing.

"You'll be civil?"

Half a smile. "I'll try my best."

A lot later than she had planned, Lee checked in on Holly and crawled between the duvet and the crisp white sheet of her bed. She stifled a yawn and pulled out her phone, remembering at the last minute that she needed to text James.

Mum's in the spare room - will explain tomorrow. No walking around naked! X

As she was typing out a second message to Beth, she received a reply from James: *But it's no clothes Tuesday! Ha. You okay?* She responded with a smiley face and a kiss, and then turned back to the message for her sister.

Mum's here, and things are better. Lunch tomorrow - the three of us? X

CHAPTER TEN

Two weeks until Christmas

It was still dark outside, but that didn't make it easy to figure out what time it was; the mornings took a long time to get light this close to Christmas, especially on days when the weather wasn't nice. Beth didn't care what time it was; she had no work that day, and she was quite happy to stay in bed for as long as was possible.

She rolled over as carefully as she could, and couldn't stop herself smiling as she looked at the muscled form of Caspian, lying next to her. Last night... Last night had been incredible.

It had been weeks since she had seen Caspian, since she had heard his voice, since she had run her fingers across his body. When she had seen him the night before, stood on the beach and looking out into the ocean, she'd barely been able to believe it. It had seemed like a dream; there had been so much that fate had needed to do to bring them to that point - although she wondered whether Mandy Blackwell had given fate a helping hand.

He had circles under his eyes that made her worry he had not been sleeping well in Edinburgh, and despite the chill in the air he slept without a stitch on. She couldn't resist running her palm across his chest, wondering whether he was swimming in the sea in Edinburgh - although to be fair, he'd said when she first met him that he only swam between April and October. And in Scotland, perhaps that window would need to be shortened a little. She'd never been, but she'd heard enough jokes about how cold it was to feel that swimming in the sea was probably not as commonplace as it was around Dartmouth.

Beth almost wanted to pinch herself. In the weeks he had been gone, she'd fallen into a funk that she'd struggled to get out of - drinking more wine than was probably sensible, spending her days off in her pyjamas in bed and trying her hardest not to think about him. She had not thought he would be in her bed again, not thought that she would get to spend the night with him.

Yes, he was still going to be living in Edinburgh.

Yes, they were going to have to do long distance.

But he was here now, and had admitted that ending things with her had most definitely been a mistake.

Beth was so pleased it was a mistake they had both been able to rectify.

They had been up a lot of the night, making up for lost time. Caspian told her about his job, about Edinburgh, about how lonely he had been without her; Beth told him about her book, her discussions with the publisher he had introduced her to, and how plans for Lee's wedding were going. They made love as if they had not seen each other in weeks; then as if they had all the time in the world. And she hoped they would do - the details could be worked out at a later date. For now they had Christmas, and they had each other. In the early hours of the morning Beth had begun to tell him about her dad, and how things had changed so much in the last few weeks.

When the light eventually began to leak in through the crack in the curtains, Beth stifled a yawn and decided to take a break from just staring at his sleeping form. She shivered as she got out from under the cosy duvet, and rummaged in a pile of clothes on the chair to find her fluffy dressing gown. She padded through to the kitchen, taking a glance back to double check that she really wasn't dreaming - he really was in her bed.

Flicking the kettle on, she scrolled through her phone and clicked on her sister's name. She wasn't quite sure how to word what had happened in the last twelve hours or so; would her sister be judgmental? Think that things wouldn't work out as they hadn't done previously? She definitely wasn't in the mood for any negativity as she floated on cloud nine.

No raining on my parade, she typed. *But Caspian is currently in my bedroom! X*

By the time her tea had brewed, her phone had beeped with a response, and she was a little hesitant to read it.

Yay! Details - not too many though - as soon as you can. I'm happy if you're happy. Xxx

Beth smiled; she shouldn't have worried. Despite their recent falling out, she knew Lee always had her best interests at heart.

I'm very happy :D x she replied, and then left her phone

on the counter to rejoin Caspian in bed with two steaming mugs and a packet of croissants.

CHAPTER ELEVEN

One week until Christmas

With mere days to go before her wedding - and Christmas - Lee felt stressed like never before. Yes, by this point everything was organised - but she kept waiting for something to go wrong. When Dartington Hall called, she presumed it was to say there was some disaster that meant their ceremony could not go ahead - when in fact it was just to confirm the numbers of vegetarian and vegan guests. When James's sister rang, she wondered if it was to announce they had some horrible bug and wouldn't be able to attend - but it was just for a chat. She didn't know why she assumed the worst, and presumed it was just her stress levels - because she was struggling to sleep too. All she wanted, she told herself in the dark as she lay awake for the third night in a row, was to be married to James without anything going wrong.

They should have just eloped.

Monday morning dawned sunny and crisp, with a thin layer of frost across the gardens and the car windscreens, and Lee made coffee to combat the effects of another disturbed night's sleep. Holly had, for once, decided to sleep in - or perhaps Lee's wake up times were getting earlier and earlier. James had been out at work for a couple of hours, and so she took her coffee back upstairs and considered getting back into bed, but there didn't seem to be much point. Holly would undoubtedly be calling out for her soon, and the day would start in earnest.

Instead, Lee opened her wardrobe and pulled out the dress she would be wearing in a few days' time; her beautiful wedding dress. It had been altered so it fit her perfectly, and she felt a sense of calm come over her now as she looked at it. Everything was organised. She had made up with Beth, and her mother, and her dad would be at the wedding. Nothing was going to go wrong, she told herself; she would wear that beautiful dress and she would become Mrs Shirley Knight, and they would have their happily-ever-after.

She was lifting the train and running her fingers round the red satin trim with a smile, being careful to keep her coffee well out of the way of the pure white satin, when she heard Holly's little voice. "Mama! Mama!"

She smiled; chaos would soon be reigning. Putting the coffee on a high shelf - she was well aware what happened to any drink in Holly's grasp - she went in to get her daughter.

When she entered the room, she immediately noticed the stain down Holly's pyjamas. "What's wrong my lovely?" she asked, darting over and immediately realising that it was sick down her top... and in her cot. "Are you okay?"

Holly babbled away as Lee tried to feel her forehead. She felt a little hot, but not burning, and Lee wondered what had caused her to be sick. She internally groaned... a sickness bug was the last thing they needed days before a wedding. And Christmas.

"Think positively," she told herself, as she lifted Holly from the cot and tried not to get the sick all over her own clothes. She stripped the pyjamas off; "She seems fine in herself. It may be nothing serious." Realising she had sick on her neck too, Lee considered bathing her, but knew that would start the day with more drama than she could handle; Holly hated the bath.

"Stay there, sweetie," she said, double checking the stair gate was safely locked across the top of the stairs and disappearing into the bathroom to get a wet flannel and a towel. A good wipe down would have to do until bath time that night.

It was then that she heard a scream.

Her heart stopped, and she dropped everything in her hands and went running. Holly's room was empty, and as she turned to face her own bedroom door she saw Holly sat on the floor, seeming to have taken a tumble but not looking seriously hurt. Lee ran to her and fussed over her hands and knees, checking carefully that the tears were only from shock and not from any actual injury. How she'd got between the rooms so quickly was a mystery, but at least she hadn't knocked her head again.

"Uh oh," Holly said when the tears had subsided, and Lee smiled.

"Uh oh indeed!" Lee said. "You need to be more careful little miss."

"Uh oh." She was looking up at the wardrobe, and when Lee turned, she realised what Holly had been holding onto when she fell.

THE BEST CHRISTMAS EVER

Her wedding dress was still on its hanger, with a jagged tear right across the waistline.

Lee sat down on the bed, mouth open in shock, and for a few moments could not think a single coherent thought.

❖ ❖ ❖

Once she'd taken Holly downstairs, plonked her in front of the telly with some cartoons and some juice and taken a very, very deep breath, Lee took out her phone and called the only person who could possibly console her at this time. Luckily, she wasn't working.

"Beth," she said, not letting her sister get a word in before beginning to talk. "Holly has ripped my dress. She must have been crawling, or walking, or cruising or something and grabbed it and fell, and with her weight... there's a huge tear. Right across the front." She didn't take a breath until she got to the end, and on the other end of the line she heard her sister taking a deep one herself.

"It might not be as bad as you think," Beth said.

"It is."

"Shall I come over?"

"Yes," Lee said. "Yes, yes, I don't know what to do..."

While she waited for her younger sister and tried not to think about the ripped wedding dress upstairs, she fixed breakfast for Holly and made herself another cup of coffee, knowing she couldn't stomach any food. Holly seemed unaware of the stress Lee felt, which she was glad about - it wasn't her fault, after all. It was just an accident.

When Beth knocked on the door, Lee let her in with Holly on her hip and took her straight upstairs to see the dress. She sat on the bed, Holly sat between her legs shaking a rattle that she had really outgrown, as Beth surveyed the damage.

"I knew something bad was going to happen," Lee said.

"No, you didn't," Beth said, examining the tear as if she knew what to do about it - which, frankly, she didn't. "This is just an accident. And I'm sure it's completely fixable."

"I feel like the whole thing is cursed," Lee whispered. "I've barely slept in days, worrying something was going to go wrong, waiting for something to go wrong, and now it has…"

Beth pulled out her phone and fired off a couple of texts before focussing back on Lee. "If you hadn't been feeling that way, then you could look at this objectively - it's an accident. It's sh- rubbish, but we can sort it out, I'm sure, and everything will go to plan."

"Holly's been sick," Lee said. "And the last few weeks… First of all I was stressed about people thinking I shouldn't be having a big wedding, and then dad reappearing, and then the fall out, and now the dress…" Tears rolled down her cheeks and she didn't do anything to stop them. "I just wish it was all over," she said in a whisper that was barely audible. "And that's not how you should feel about your wedding day. I've messed up a marriage once already. I don't want to do it again…"

Beth lifted her niece off the bed, put her on her hip and took Lee by the hand. She led her downstairs, and placed

Holly in front of the cartoons on the telly despite Lee's pro-tests. "A day of too many cartoons is not going to damage her for Life. Now listen to me."

She led Lee into the hallway, where she could deliver the much needed pep-talk without worrying about Holly overhearing any bad words or negativity. "You have just let stress get the better of you. You work two jobs - run two businesses, I should say - take care of a one-year-old, you're planning a wedding and hosting Christmas for a million. It's no wonder you're stressing, or worrying about things going wrong - but you can't let it ruin things, Lee. You are over-thinking this. Answer me this: do you love James?"

Lee nodded. "Of course I do."

"Do you want to marry him?"

Again, Lee nodded.

"Then the rest is gravy. I'm serious. You can cancel the whole thing if you like, go to a registry office and be done with it - but I don't think that's what you really want."

Lee shook her head.

"Everything has snowballed, and with all the crap that's happened in the last few weeks - I mean, the last twenty years has turned out to be full of lies, that's pretty big news - I can understand. But you've got to stop that snowball getting any bigger. The only snow we want is on Christmas Day - and maybe your wedding day too, hey?"

With a small smile, Lee wiped her tears with a sleeve and took a deep breath.

"You're right. I know you are."

"Of course I am," Beth said with a grin. "Now, you need sleep and you need to switch off from everything. And if you can, I think you need to take a few days off work, book in a manicure and a facial and focus on having a wonderful wedding." Her phone beeped and Beth glanced at it, her smile widening.

"I guess I could…"

"You're the boss, do it. But for now, you're going to go and have a nap, and I'm going to sort everything out. Yes, I'll look after Holly - are you happy for me to drive with her?"

Lee nodded. "You'll need her car seat - so maybe just take my car. Can I ask where you're going?"

"Nope," Beth said.

"She might be sick again…"

"Then I'll clean it up. Hey, it'll be in your car anyway. Go. Bed. It'll all look better after some sleep."

Lee really was exhausted, and so she nodded, gave Holly a kiss and told her to be good, and disappeared to her bedroom, only raising her eyebrows when Beth followed her up and took the ruined wedding dress.

"Don't ask," she said. "Sleep!"

Beth glanced in the back as she pulled up outside Mandy Blackwell's house. Her boyfriend's (she was still thrilled to think of him as that in her head) mother was someone she had only met three times, but when Caspian had replied to her woe-filled messages saying to take the dress to his mother, she hadn't needed to be told twice. Holly had drifted off in the car seat, and hadn't shown any other signs of being sick - although Beth had stored the dress on the front seat, as far away from her as possible, just to be safe.

With a bit of difficulty, she managed to pick up the sleeping child and drape the dress over her arm, and she hurried to the front door before the heavens decided to open as the black clouds seemed to be threatening. Thankfully Mandy opened the door quickly, and instantly took the torn dress off her before ushering her in.

"Thanks for this, Mandy," she said, following her into the living room.

"Not a problem at all!" she said with a smile. "And who's this little lovely?"

"My niece, Holly," Beth said, setting her down on the sofa and marvelling at how heavy a little girl could be. "Sorry for bringing her, but the dress tearing was a bit of a final straw situation - I think my sister just needed a break!"

Mandy smoothed the dress out on the table and began to inspect the damage. "No problem at all. And can I just say how pleased I am things have worked out between you and my Caspian? I've never seen him so happy."

Beth blushed. "I'm very happy too," she said.

"I said it would all work out. Now, let's see if we can't sort this out for your sister."

"Caspian said you were a bit of a whizz with a sewing machine," Beth said.

Mandy laughed; "He flatters me," she said. "But I can certainly use one, so I'll give it my best shot. Do you want to go and put the kettle on? I'll keep an eye on the little one."

An hour and two cups of tea later, Mandy took off her glasses and held up the dress to the dimming light from the window. Beth stood up to have a proper look, making sure first that there were no biscuit crumbs or traces of chocolate on her fingers.

"That's incredible, Mandy!" she said, staring at where the tear had been. "I wouldn't even know it had been damaged!"

"Well, I don't know about that, but I had some similar lace, so that helps to make it all look a little smoother. Hopefully your sister will be happy."

"She'll be over the moon!" She threw her arms around Mandy in an exuberant hug, which the older lady returned. Holly's eyes began to flicker open, and Beth turned as she began to wail.

"It's okay sweetie, Auntie Beth's here! Don't worry, we're going to go home and see mummy." She helped the little girl off the sofa, and lifted her up into her arms. "I can't thank you enough, Mandy. Let me give you some money, at least for your materials-"

"Don't be ridiculous," Mandy said, batting her hand away. "Just let me know how your sister's big day goes. I want to see plenty of photos of you and Caspian!"

Mandy helped her out to the car with the dress and the toddler, and once they were all strapped in and waving goodbye, the sun began to peek out from behind the clouds. Beth grinned, feeling like everything truly was going to be okay.

◆ ◆ ◆

There were a lot of introductions as the various family members of both Lee and James gathered in a pub at the bottom of Totnes high street. It was the same pub, in fact, that Lee had stayed in when she'd fled from Bristol and her cheating ex-husband, and so the place held some nostalgia for her. Some of the family members had not met in the two years they had been together; and Beth's mother had not yet met Caspian.

They arrived together, hand in hand, and Beth took a deep breath before heading over to the assembled group in the corner of the room.

"Mothers love me," Caspian whispered to her, and she couldn't help but laugh at that.

"I hope so," she muttered.

She greeted her sister first, giving her a hug and letting Lee once again thank her and Caspian for the saving of her dress. Tina Davis was stood a couple of metres away, glass of wine in hand and having a fairly relaxed-looking conversation with James's mum. They'd all met the previous year at an eventful Easter lunch where Lee had announced she was pregnant.

"Hi, mum," she said. "Mrs Knight."

"Call me Sadie," she said, leaning over to kiss her on the cheek. "I told you!" She was called by one of her children and disappeared with apologies, and Beth turned to her mother.

"This is Caspian, mum. My boyfriend." She grinned at the word, and glanced up at Caspian, pleased to see he was smiling too. "This is my mum, Tina Davis."

"Lovely to meet you, Mrs Davis," he said in his smooth, deep voice. He held out his hand to shake hers, which she took after a second's hesitation.

"It's nice to meet you, Caspian," she said. "What an unusual name!"

He smiled; "My mum loves the sea," he said by way of explanation.

"I've always liked unusual names," she said. "Not that my children appreciate that!"

"I love the name Elizabeth," he said, and just like that, a conversation was struck up. Beth watched them, open-mouthed, as they sat together at the bar and began to chat about Caspian's line of work and where Tina lived. Clearly he was right - mothers did love him.

When she felt it was safe, she disappeared to the bar to get them both a drink, and Lee appeared at her shoulder.

"You've left him alone with mum? Is that wise?" she asked with a laugh.

"I know... but they seem to be getting on. Terrifying thought..."

"Stranger things have happened!" she said, ordering her own drinks and putting Beth's on the tab with them. She sighed; "I still feel bad about not inviting dad tonight."

"Like you said," Beth answered, carrying the two glasses

of wine carefully, "It would have been awkward, and that's not what you need. He's coming tomorrow, and he's thrilled about that."

"If I could have your attention," James said, standing to face the very large table of their assembled family. "I'd just like to say a couple of words. I'm not usually the one who does the talking," he said, and everyone laughed and glanced at a blushing Lee. "But I thought I should give it a go on this occasion." He was wearing the pale blue jumper she had bought for him on her bridesmaid dress shopping trip with Beth, and Lee loved how it brought out his eyes.

"Tomorrow," he said, "I get to marry the love of my life." There were a few 'awws' from the family members present, and Lee blushed even pinker - but smiled broadly. "And I just wanted to thank you all for coming to celebrate with us. I know for some of you it's been more of a journey than others, and we appreciate all of you for all your help in getting to this point, your saving of the wedding dress-" he lifted his glass towards Beth, who laughed from her position between Caspian and Lee, "-your shopping advice and everything else in between." He paused, and smiled at his almost-wife. "Christmas is a very important time for us. We met at Christmas, fell in love over Christmas, named our daughter after a festive plant..." There was laughter from the group. "And so getting married at Christmas seemed the obvious choice. What we did not think about was how much more stressful Christmas would be with a wedding days before it, or how much busier we would both be with work right before Christmas! So I want to thank Lee, for everything she's done to make tomorrow what I know will be a perfect day."

"I feel very lucky to be surrounded by so many family members the night before we get married, and so this toast is to you all - and to true love."

They raised their glasses and cheered as James kissed his bride-to-be. Despite the fact that the wedding was tomorrow, Lee felt like all her stresses had melted away. Beth was right; what mattered was that she loved James and wanted to marry him. The rest, as Beth so eloquently put it, was gravy. The fact that Caspian's mother had managed to save her dress so it didn't look like anything had ever befallen it - well, that was just the cherry on the very sweet cake.

"I love you, Mr Knight," she said, pressing her lips to his once more.

"I love you too, Ms Davis," he said, and she grinned. Tomorrow, the three of them would be Knights, and everything would be as she knew it should be.

Beth reclined against Caspian's sturdy form in the chair behind her, watching as Holly and her cousin Jasper played together. Well, really they played alongside each other, occasionally grabbing each other's toys, but it was cute to watch. James's brother had agreed to watch over the two of them that evening, so James and Lee could be carefree on the night before their wedding. In the actual wedding ceremony, Beth and her mum were in charge of Holly, who would then be going to James's sister for the rest of the day. As it was with everything Lee did, there was a plan of action.

THE BEST CHRISTMAS EVER

"They seem very happy," Caspian said, speaking quietly just to Beth as the other family members broke off into smaller groups to chat. He didn't really know anyone here, other than having met Lee a couple of times, but then Beth didn't really either - James's family was far larger than her own.

"They do," Beth said with a grin. "They're perfect together - I'm just so glad they found each other. Imagine there being someone out there who's perfect for you and you never find them?"

"You're a romantic," Caspian said with a smile. "Sounds like soul mates and fate you're talking about."

"Maybe I am," Beth said, turning in her chair to face him. "Do you mind if I'm a romantic?"

"Not in the slightest," Caspian said, and, not caring about who might witness it, pressed his lips against hers for just a second. Long enough to make her cheeks blush red; not quite long enough for her to forget that they were in a public place.

"Good," she said, leaning back with a contented smile and watching her sister happily chatting away with her future in-laws.

CHAPTER TWELVE

The wedding

"This is it," Lee said, taking a deep breath and turning to her sister, the only one close enough to hear her in the little atrium before entering the hall. There was a low hum of chatter within the thick oak double doors, and although she wasn't yet late, Lee worried the assembled family and friends would begin to get restless.

"You ready?" Beth asked, reaching over and straightening a wisp of Lee's blonde hair that looked dangerously close to getting stuck to her eyelash. She gave her sister's hand a squeeze, noticing it was shaking just slightly.

Lee gulped. "Yes. Yes, I am."

"Take a deep breath," Beth said, hearing a slight tremor to her sister's voice that she knew was just nerves. "This is your day. It is going to be amazing. You look incredible, Lee. James won't know what hit him."

Lee grinned. "Thank you. Not just for today - but for everything you've done for this wedding. The organising, the decorating, the talking me down off a ledge…"

"Shh. We're not even going to mention that today. This is the right man for you. This marriage is going to work. This is the start of the rest of your life, Lee."

Lee gave her sister a quick hug, careful not to crush either of their dresses. "You are, of course, one hundred per cent right."

"As always. I'm going to give the signal - this is it!"

Beth stepped through the double doors and indicated that they were ready, returning seconds later carrying Lee's one-year-old daughter, Holly. Both Beth and Holly were in matching shades of red, with tartan sashes. Holly's was accompanied with thick white tights and a holly-themed headband, and she smiled and held her arms out for Lee as soon as she saw her.

"Hello my sweetheart," Lee said, giving her daughter a cuddle but letting Beth keep hold of her. "You're going to walk down the aisle with Auntie Beth! And don't you both look beautiful."

"Not as beautiful as the bride," Beth said, taking her place in front of Lee with Holly on her hip. Beth's dress was the same crimson, with a v-shaped neckline in delicate red lace. Instead of a headband, she wore a holly-themed bracelet, and she had left her holly, rose and pine-cone bouquet at the front of the hall, to be held once she had passed the real Holly to their mother.

The music started up - an instrumental version of 'All I Want for Christmas is You' - and Lee felt her lips curve into a smile as those double doors opened. The bridesmaids went first - Gina, Janet, Therese, Tamsin and then Beth, and Lee heard the oohs and ahhs that her infant daughter was attracting from the crowd. She couldn't quite see James from her vantage point, and so when she heard her cue, she was desperate to step out and see the man that she was so ready to marry.

Everyone stood and turned to face her as she stepped onto the red carpet that ran the length of the hall. At the end of each pew were sprigs of holly and mistletoe, all designed to bring the magic of the season that Lee loved the most; the magic of the season that had brought her and James together two years ago.

Her dress was the traditional white, but with a red satin ribbon trim around the train, and the same around the waist. It was covered in a layer of lace and sequins, which caught the light from the chandeliers and looked like the sparkle of frost on a winter's night. That tear that had threatened to ruin everything was hidden from sight, just another intricate piece of lace in a beautiful work of art.

Lee had elected to walk down the aisle alone; she was after all a divorcee, a mother, and over thirty. Considering the fact that she had not seen her father for so many years, she hadn't felt it was right for him to be the one to accompany her, and although her mother had walked her down the aisle for her first wedding, she'd decided she wanted to do this on her own. She had worried about offending her mother, of course, but since moving down to Devon in a whirlwind just over two years ago, she was learning to think about herself a little more and worry about offending others a little less. She passed her father, a few rows in from the back, smiling proudly alongside a red-haired gentleman she presumed was his husband, and for a moment she caught his eye with a grin before turning her attention back to the end of the aisle.

And there, at the end of the red carpet, stood next to his brother John who was standing as his best man, and with Beth stood waiting on the other side, he stood. Tall, with short, curly hair that never looked completely tamed and with his hands behind his back, stood the man she was about to marry. Her eyes met his and she found herself tuning out the rest of the room, focussing only on those eyes, on that smile, on the slightly nervous look that played on his face. His suit was black, with a red waistcoat and matching cravat, and of course he had a sprig of holly in his buttonhole. For a second, Lee tore her eyes away from her handsome groom and sought out her daughter in the front row, sat on grandma's lap, happily playing with the brooch that was pinned to her red dress. Their Holly; their little surprise that had sped up their relationship in so many ways.

Not today though; today they had all the time to be James and Lee, in love. Christmas, a time of year Lee had always felt had magic in the air - and now she felt that magic was surrounding them in the picturesque, antique hall, as she reached the man she loved.

"Hey," he murmured, and her smile widened.

"Hey."

She turned and passed her own bouquet - a larger version of the one Beth had collected from the front of the church - to her sister, and lost herself in James' gaze.

"Please be seated," the officiant called, and the scraping of wood on stone floor could be heard as everyone settled in to see the magic unfolding before their eyes.

CHAPTER THIRTEEN

Epilogue - Christmas Day

"Merry Christmas!" Beth shouted as Lee opened the door. She seemed to have sequins in her hair - something which Beth presumed Holly was responsible for - and had an apron around her waist.

"Merry Christmas!" Lee said back, hugging her sister and then Caspian.

"This is my mum, Mandy," he said. "This is Beth's sister Lee."

"Thank you so much for having me," Mandy said; when Beth had said she was bailing out of Christmas at Lee's so she could spend it with Caspian and his mum, Lee had insisted that two more wouldn't make much of a difference, and that she wanted to spend Christmas with all the family.

"Thank you for saving my wedding dress!" Lee countered, moving out the way to let them in. "It's a bit like musical chairs I'm afraid, but if you glare at someone you might get them to give theirs up for you!"

Wonderful smells of food cooking came from the kitchen, and Beth shouted through to James as she hung up her coat. Despite Lee wearing an apron, Beth knew full well her sister would not be doing the bulk of the cooking.

The living room was, as Lee had said, rather packed, and Beth laughed at Holly and Jasper sat in a pile of sequins on the floor.

"*Somebody* decided it would be a good idea to put sequins in every package for Holly to open," Lee said, with a roll of her eyes but a smile on her lips. "I won't name names," she whispered, "But they may not be invited again next year!"

"Oops," Beth said with a laugh, wondering which of the guests was responsible. The fire was roaring away, next to a real Christmas tree that practically glittered with lights, tinsel and decorations on every available twig. The presents that had not yet been opened were stacked beneath it, and every chair was taken - although James's brother immediately offered his up to Mrs Blackwell and joined his son on the floor.

There were many choruses of 'Happy Christmas', and Mandy commented on how perfect the cottage was - "Like the front of a Christmas card!"

"The first year I came here, it was snowing," she said. "It did really look like some festive scene on a card then - you couldn't believe it was a real house!"

Beth disappeared to talk with her mother; Caspian took a seat on the floor.

"So," James's mother asked. "How is married life?"

"Chaotic!" Lee said. "Although that might have something to do with having a one-year-old and it being Christmas. Ask me in the new year!"

They all laughed. "And are you going on honeymoon?"

Tamsin, James's sister-in-law asked.

"We've booked to go skiing, in February," Lee said. "Just for three days. Holly is going to stay with Sadie and Mark, and we're going skiing in France - which I've never done!"

As John shared his disastrous first skiing trip story, Lee snuck into the kitchen.

"All going okay?" she asked.

"Yep," he answered, stirring something vigorously. "All okay with the family?"

She nodded. "No drama - yet!"

James pointed to the beam above and grinned. "Mistletoe."

"I wonder how that got there!" Lee said with a grin, stepping forward to press a long kiss to her husband's lips.

❖ ❖ ❖

"I know we've had a lot of speeches this week," James's dad said, to the crowded room of people. They laughed appreciatively. "But I hope you'll indulge me one more. First of all, to the cook-" They raised their glasses in James's direction. "It was delicious, and the fact that you catered for so many of us is a miracle."

"Hear hear."

"I feel very lucky, this Christmas," he said. "I'm surrounded by family - close and extended - and I have a new daughter-in-law. Two beautiful grandchildren, and enough Christmas pudding to sink a battleship. It is a truly magical time of year, and the love in this room makes that all the more apparent. I hope for many, many more Christmases like this one - and perhaps a few more grandchildren too!"

There was collective laughter as they joined Mark Knight in raising their glasses.

"Here's to the best Christmas ever."

"The best Christmas ever!"

Thank you so much for reading! The story continues in 'Trouble in Tartan': mybook.to/troubleintartan

Eager to see more of Beth and Caspian's story? Read on for a sneak-peak of book 5 in the series, 'Trouble in Tartan'.

TROUBLE
IN TARTAN:
CHAPTER ONE

"Hogmanay?" Beth said, as she tried to stretch out her legs in the window seat of the aeroplane. "Am I saying it right?"

Caspian nodded. His legs were even more squashed than hers - especially since he had insisted she have the window seat, and so he was stuck in the middle - and his thigh was pressed against Beth's. She certainly wasn't complaining. After they had separated for months, she had spent every moment possible with him over the festive period - and when he'd suggested coming to celebrate the New Year in Edinburgh with him, she'd jumped at the chance. "It's a big deal in Scotland, so I hear," he said, stretching an arm and wrapping it around her shoulders. She snuggled in and grinned to herself as she looked out over the thick clouds below them.

"Bigger than everywhere else?"

"Well, this will be my first time experiencing it too, but from what I hear it is. They even have another bank holiday after New Year's Day, to recover!"

"That sounds like an excellent idea," Beth said.

"We've got two options," Caspian said. "For the actual night. Stay in and watch the fireworks from my flat - clothes totally optional... or I guess we could go to the big party on Princes Street. I mean, I did get tickets, just in case."

Beth turned and pressed her lips to his, paying no heed to the disapproving looks from the elderly man in the aisle seat. "As much as I love the sound of clothes-optional fire-works," she said with a grin that was enough to make Caspian blush; "I feel like the party on Princes Street is a once-in-a-lifetime sort of a thing. Whereas, I hope, nights in with you are going to be pretty frequent..."

He kissed the top of her head as she rested it against his shoulder. "As frequent as they can be in a long-distance re-lationship spanning 500 miles!"

Beth groaned. "Don't remind me. I've got used to spend-ing time with you again, since we got back together..."

"Let's just enjoy ourselves, with the time we've got then," Caspian said. "We've got a week until your flight home. And we'll book in the next visit before you even go - that'll make it seem sooner."

Beth sighed. "It all sounds so romantic..." she said. "Until I actually have to get on the plane and leave."

*   *   *

They took a tram from the airport to Haymarket, then dashed across the road and jumped on a bus to save walk-ing to Caspian's flat in the rapidly cooling evening air. Beth giggled and pulled on Caspian's hand, dragging him up the stairs to the top floor of the double decker. They managed to snag the front seats - there were only three other people up there - and Beth squashed in next to the window. Caspian placed their bags on a seat behind them and folded his long legs into the small space.

"Feels like we're driving the bus," Beth said, and her smile was infectious.

Caspian threw an arm round her, feeling the happiest he had felt in this city since moving here. He knew full well why that was - and he was trying not to dwell on the fact that it would come to an end in not that long.

"Were you a back seat rebel?" she asked, "You know, back in school?"

Caspian laughed. "Not sure I've ever been a rebel."

"I don't believe that. I can imagine you... sexy, moody teenager, secrets to hide, a mysterious air about you..."

"Not so sure about that," he said with a smile. "I was the quiet kid who was good at English and hated PE."

"Really?" she said, closing one eye and appraising him. "With those muscles, I thought you'd be a whiz at PE." She gave his arm a squeeze to prove her point.

"The muscles came later," he said. "I told you - cancer scare, wake up call, blah, blah, blah. Before then there were far fewer muscles! You probably wouldn't have even noticed me."

She glanced into his warm brown eyes and ran her fingers through the strands of hair that threatened to fall in

120

front of his eyes. "I think I would have done."

"And you?" he asked with a smile. "Outspoken, rebel teenager? Dyed hair, different boyfriend every week?"

"That's how you see me, is it?" she said, laughing so loudly the gentleman four rows back looked up from his phone. "Fairly outspoken, I guess, although no dyed hair - my mum wouldn't let me! And the boyfriends weren't quite as numerous as you make it sound."

"Yeah, yeah. I'd have been one in a long line of admirers, I bet."

"You think you'd have admired me?" Beth said.

"Of course."

She pressed her lips against his, feeling like a teenager again, making out on a bus without a care in the world who saw her.

As the rain started, the bus pulled up to a bus stop, and it was only as it was about to leave that Caspian broke from the kiss and realised it was their stop.

"Wait!" Beth shouted, as Caspian grabbed their bags and they dashed down the steps, Beth almost tripping at the bottom.

"Sorry!" Caspian shouted as the bus driver tutted. Beth wound her hand through the crook of his elbow, and they dashed through the rain, darting across the road just as the lights were about to turn, and quickly found themselves in the stairwell that led up to his flat.

"That rain seemed to come out of nowhere!"

Caspian laughed; "Seems that's what it's like up here - sunshine one minute, rain the next."

The trudged up the stairs, dripping wet, Caspian still carrying all the bags and Beth just contending with her handbag and her soaking raincoat. As Caspian unlocked the door, Beth looked around at the other flats, all with strange numbering conventions; 1F1, 1F2... it wasn't like any flats she'd seen in England. Even in the hallway the ceilings were high, and as they walked through the doorway she could see why Caspian liked the place. It felt old, and sturdy, and full of history - but the storage heaters kept it cosy, and the large bay windows gave a great view of the busy street below.

Once Caspian had dumped the bags in the bedroom, Beth had made her way into the living room. He ran a hand through his dark hair, water droplets falling from it, and gave Beth a shy smile.

"It's nice to have you here," he said.

"It's nice to be here," Beth said, taking a step towards him. "But don't you think we should get out of these wet clothes?"

Caspian grinned. "I wouldn't want you getting ill, not on your very first visit to Scotland."

Another step closer.

"That would really ruin the new year," Beth said, crossing over her arms and pulling her t-shirt over her head, dumping it on the floor.

Caspian took a step closer, and then his warm hands

were on her bare waist, the heat emanating from them making the goosebumps subside. She was amazed still at the feelings this man could stir up in her; even tired and soaked, she just wanted to feel his skin against hers. The months they had spent apart had only intensified that longing - perhaps it would be the same with their long-distance relationship.

"We can't have that," he said, pulling his own t-shirt from his body and adding it to the pile on the floor, then pressing his lips to the delicate flesh just below her ear, causing her to groan.

"Caspian..." she whispered, her fingers grasping his wet hair, and then she let out a giggle as he easily lifted her, carrying her off to the bedroom next door.

*   *   *

Beth's eyes fluttered open, and she took a second to remember where she was, before rolling over to see Caspian's sleeping form next to her, and grinning. They had obviously both fallen asleep, but the rumbling in her stomach had woken her and she very much hoped Caspian had a plan for dinner.

It was dark outside, but she could see Caspian's alarm clock on the other side of the bed, showing it was nearly eight o'clock. As he breathed steadily in and out, she snuck out of the bed, threw on his dressing gown (which was neatly hung on the back of the door) and padded to the kitchen. It was a long, thin room with a tall fridge-freezer and very clean surfaces - just as she would have expected. When she opened the fridge, she was disappointed to find it fairly empty, save for some butter, cheese and milk. At least tea was possible, she thought, flicking the kettle on and wandering to the living room.

The bay windows looked out onto the busy street below. Several of the flats opposite had their lights on, and she could see Christmas trees still lit in people's living rooms, as well as lights strung up in front of shops in the distance. It was a very different place to Dartmouth, that was for sure; she loved her flat that overlooked the water, the way she knew so many people when she walked down the high street, the laid back nature of most of the residents. But she could see the appeal here too; it was so vibrant, so exciting, more so than anywhere she had lived before. In the back of her mind there was the thought that she could have been living here - he'd asked her. She'd said no. It was for good reasons, she knew that; but as she snuggled into his dressing gown, knowing he was asleep just metres away, and looked out over the bustling city, it was hard not to have some doubts.

She jumped as strong arms wrapped around her waist, before smiling and leaning back into Caspian's embrace.

"You scared me!"

"You looked very lost in thought," he said, pressing a kiss to the bare skin of her neck.

"Are you not cold?" she asked, deflecting a little, as she turned and saw he was only in his boxers - something which she certainly appreciated.

He smiled. "Someone stole my robe."

"Oops." She laughed. "So, what's the plan for dinner? I'm afraid I'm starving…"

"I thought a takeaway," Caspian said. "The fridge is rather empty - as I'm sure you've already seen - but we can go out if you like. Although that would mean getting dressed..."

She trailed her fingers down his bare chest and giggled.

"A takeaway sounds perfect."

Available now on Amazon: mybook.to/troubleintartan

AFTERWORD

Thank you so much for reading 'The Best Christmas Ever'! I hope you enjoyed catching up with Lee, James, Beth and Caspian and their large collection of family and friends. I'm excited to have shared their wedding with you, and a little more Christmas magic!

This isn't the last you'll hear of the South West Series. The next novel will focus on Beth and Caspian's relationship - and is available on Amazon (mybook.to/troubleintartan)!

To hear about new releases, see pictures of my dog and generally hear about my writing, you can sign up to my newsletter here: tiny.cc/paulinyi

Reviews are really appreciated, and make a huge difference to indie authors - so if you can review, please do! You can also get in touch by emailing me at rebeccapaulinyi@gmail.com

You can read Lee and James's story in 'The Worst Christmas Ever?' (mybook.to/worstchristmas) and 'Lawyers and Lattes' (mybook.to/lawyersandlattes). Read about Beth and Caspian's relationship in 'Feeling the Fireworks' (mybook.to/feelingthefireworks) and 'Trouble in Tartan' (mybook.to/troubleintartan).

The sixth book in the series, 'Summer of Sunshine', revists all the characters: mybook.to/summerofsunshine ! And keep an eye ou tofr book seven, where we meet Caspian's cousing Isla: mybook.to/healingtheheartbreak.

BOOKS IN THIS SERIES

The South West Series

Love, laughter and new beginnings in rural South West England.

The Worst Christmas Ever?

Can the magic of the Christmas season be rediscovered in a small Devon town?

When Shirley 'Lee' Jones returns home from an awful day at the office, the last thing she expects to find is her husband in bed with another woman. Six weeks until Christmas, and Lee finds the life she had so carefully planned has been utterly decimated.

Hurt, angry and confused, Lee makes a whirlwind decision to drive her problems away and ends up in Totnes, an eccentric town in the heart of Devon. As Christmas approaches, Lee tries to figure out what path her life will follow now, as she looks at it from the perspective of a soon-to-be 31-year-old divorcée.

Can she ever return to her normal life? Or is a new reality - and a new man - on the horizon?

Finding herself and flirting with the handsome local police officer might just make this the best Christmas ever.

Lawyers And Lattes

A new home, a new man, and a new career are all great - but do they always lead to happily-ever-after?

Shirley 'Lee' Jones has made some spontaneous and sometimes questionable decisions since the breakup of her marriage, but deciding to remain in the quirky town of Totnes has got to be the biggest decision so far. Now Lee has a new business, gorgeous man, and friends keeping life interesting. But when questions of law crop up in her life again, she finds herself yearning for the career and the life plan she gave up when she left everything behind.

And when unexpected news tests her relationship, her resolve, and everything tying her to her life, Lee must decide between the person she is and the person she wants to become.

Sometimes decisions about life, law, and love all reside in grey areas. Will Lee's newfound happiness in Devon be short-lived? Or could her new life give her the chance to have everything she's ever wanted?

Feeling The Fireworks

Can Beth rekindle her passion for life and love in picturesque Dartmouth?

When Beth Davis made a whirlwind decision to move to

picturesque Dartmouth to shake up her repetitive life, the last thing she expected to find was a passion in life - or a man who could make her feel fireworks.

A change in home and job seems like exactly what Beth needs to blow away the cobwebs that have been forming around her dead-end job. With little money to her name and no real plan, Beth needs to make things work, fast - without relying on her big sister Lee to bail her out.

When she meets the handsome, mysterious Caspian in a daring late-night swim, she instantly feels fireworks that she had long forgotten. Can Dartmouth - and Caspian - re-awaken her passion for life and love?

'Feeling the Fireworks' is Book 3 in the South West Series but can be read as a standalone novel. Fall in love with Devon today!

The Best Christmas Ever

A Devon wedding with the magic of Christmas and a dose of small town charm - and the potential for a lot of family drama.

Lee Davis is about to marry the man of her dreams - and at her favourite time of year. But she's finding it hard to feel the magic of Christmas or the excitement about her wedding as a face from her past reappears and worries about her second time down the aisle surface.

James Knight thought he had everything - the woman he was destined to be with, an adorable daughter and a happy life in the countryside. But with his wife-to-be seeming more and more distant, is he doomed to be jilted at the alter again?

Beth Davis is pretty sure she's lost her heart to handsome, brooding Caspian - but he's moved away to Edinburgh, and their fiery romance seems to have been stopped before it had truly started.

Caspian Blackwell wants to be excited about his promotion and moving to an vibrant new city - but his heart is very much back in Dartmouth.

Can a festive Devon wedding make this the Best Christmas Ever?

Trouble In Tartan

Beth Davis didn't plan on falling in love when she moved to Dartmouth - she just wanted to feel some fireworks. The problem is, she's pretty sure that is exactly what is happening - but the object of her affections is living 600 miles away in Edinburgh. As she tries to start a career as an author, downs a few too many glasses of wine and attempts to make ends meet, keeping a long-distance relationship alive proves more and more challenging.

Caspian Blackwell has never let his heart make big decisions - but he's sorely tempted when the distance between them begins to cause problems in his relationship with Beth. When he decides he wants all or nothing, can he really put this new relationship before his career? Or will he end up exactly where he always feared he would: heartbroken?

A tale of love, longing and a relationship stretched between coastal England and Scotland.

Summer Of Sunshine

A summer holiday can wash up a whole host of family dramas...

Lee Knight wants to relax on a summer holiday away with her husband, sister and brother-in-law. But her desire for another baby is not making it easy to unwind.

James Knight hates to see his wife upset, and hopes a trip away will make her troubles lessen. But with concerns about his father's health, he's finding it hard to be there for her as much as she really needs.

Beth Blackwell is sick to death of everyone asking her two questions: when is her next book coming out, and when is she going to have a baby. The first is proving more difficult than she expected, and the second - well, she's not sure whether that's the way she wants her life to go.

Caspian Blackwell is enjoying life as a newlywed in Edinburgh - although in his heart, he's missing living in Devon. A spate of redundancies at work has him pondering his future - but he worries his new wife's heart is engaged elsewhere when she becomes increasingly distant.

Can sun, sea and sand send the two couples back into more harmonious waters?

Healing The Heartbreak

Isla Blackwell thought she knew what love was.

But when her five year relationship ends in heartbreak, no home, and no job, she decides to take up her cousin's offer of a break in beautiful coastal Devon.

She expects sea, sand and perhaps some confort for her shattered soul - but when she starts taking shifts at a local bookshop, could love be on the cards?

With the guidance of her cousin Caspian and the rest of his family, as well as the handsome Luca, can Isla heal her broken heart?

'Healing the Heartbreak' is Book Seven in 'The South West Series', but can be read as a standalone novel.

BOOKS BY THIS AUTHOR

The Love Of A Lord

When grieving hearts find each other, can love overcome secrets, vows and society's expectations?

Compelled to uncover the secret surrounding her mother's death, Annelise Edwards unexpectedly finds herself the guest of the handsome Lord Gifford.

Lord Nicholas Gifford has no interest in women after being jilted by his betrothed, but he cannot ignore his sense of duty when a mysterious woman appears on his doorstep during a terrible storm and falls ill.

As they wait for the storm and Annelise's fever to pass, they are forced to share the grief that is weighing on both their hearts. And when Nicholas becomes more involved in Annelise's efforts to piece together her mother's past, it becomes increasingly difficult to deny their blooming attraction.

Will Nicholas give up the lonely life he has become accustomed to? And will it even matter once he finds out Annelise's mother was nothing but their maid?

If you like your rags to riches romance mixed with Tudor drama, you'll love this heart-warming first novel in the touching The Hearts of Tudor England series.

The Love of a Lord is book one in The Hearts of Tudor England series, and can be read as a standalone novel.

Can't Let My Heart Fall

When a marriage is arranged for Alice and Christopher, love was never part of the bargain.

Alice Page long ago swore she would never fall in love. After watching her father's heartbreak at the death of her mother, and Queen Katherine's pain at her husband's philandering, it just doesn't seem worth the pain.

Marriage to Christopher Danley, however, makes keeping that solemn vow to herself somewhat difficult. In the daytime she can keep her distance, but at night she realises she has never felt closer to another human before.

Lord Christopher 'Kit' Danley knows he will be an Earl one day, but he plans to spend every moment of the time before that happens travelling the seas and discovering new lands. When his father delivers an ultimatum, marriage is the only option – but never did he imagine he would find marriage as enjoyable as he does with Lady Alice.

With Alice panicking at realising her heart may be lost to the handsome Kit Danley, and Kit called away on the King's business, can love flourish in this marriage of convenience?

Can't Let My Heart Fall is book two in The Hearts of Tudor England series, and can be read as a standalone novel.

Misrule My Heart

When Isabel realises over the Twelve Days of Christmas that she cannot marry the man she is required to, will she follow her family's wishes or her heart's desires?

Isabel Radcliffe knows she must marry well. As the daughter of a merchant who has risen at court, many opportunities are within her grasp - and marrying a Lord is one of them.

When her father hosts nobility over the Twelve Days of Christmas, she knows she will meet the man he wishes her to marry, and begin the life that has been laid out before her.

What she does not expect is for him to be quite so old or quite so unpleasant...

Suddenly, the duty binding her to such a life-changing decision feels like too much of a sacrifice. And when her head and heart are turned by the dashing and daring stable lad Avery, she questions whether she can follow through with her father's wishes.

A tale of love, duty and the magic of Christmas, with a dose of Tudor drama.

Misrule My Heart is book three in 'The Hearts of Tudor England' series, and can be read as a standalone novel.

Saving Grace's Heart

Since witnessing her sister's romantic elopement, Grace Radcliffe has been determined to choose her own husband.

And while finding excuses not to marry every man her father has put in her path has worked so far, she knows time is not on her side - and so she sets her sights on the handsome Duke of Lincoln, planning to ensure they are a good match before letting her father seal the deal.

When Harry, the dashing new Duke of Leicester, is put in her path instead, she knows there must be something wrong with him - for her father has never picked well in the past.

But when he helps her in her hour of greatest need, she begins to question that judgement.

Can Grace find the route to true love? Or will her free-spirited ways lead her into a loveless marriage?

Saving Grace's Heart is Book Four in 'The Hearts of Tudor England' Series, and can be read as a standalone novel.

Learning To Love Once More

A widowed Earl, a lonely governess, and a whole lot of heartbreak.

James, Earl of Tetbury, has never known an all-consuming love - but after losing his wife to the perils of childbirth, he resolved not to suffer that pain again.

Fed up of being a burden on her Aunt and Uncle, orphaned Catherine Thompkins decides being a governess will fill the loneliness in her soul and provide her with a modicum of independence. What she is not expecting is to fall in love with the Earl she is working for.

When James realises he and the children need Catherine in order to flourish, he offers marriage - but in name only. There will be no more children, he is resolute about that.

As Catherine falls deeper and deeper in love with the damaged Earl, can she persuade him that love is worth risking your heart for?

Learning to Love Once More is Book Five in 'The Hearts of Tudor England' series, and can be read as a standalone novel.

An Innocent Heart

On the same day as Henry VIII's second daughter is born, Elizabeth Beaufort makes her way into the world. Inspired by the way the Princess lives her life, she vows to live as a maid - no love, no marriage, no children.

But as the Tudor dynasty sends lives in England reeling, can Bessie Beaufort's heart remain caged?

Edward Ferrers has always known he will marry and carry on his father's merchant business. In fact, such a marriage has been lined up for him for several years - until a chance meeting at the Tudor Court sends his heart racing for Bessie Beaufort.

In a time of courtly love, female purity and religious upset, can Edward persuade Bessie that their love is worth fighting for?

An Innocent Heart is Book Six in 'The Hearts of Tudor England' series, and can be read as a standalone novel.

Let Love Grow

Lady Lily Merriweather has waited a long time for love to blossom. Through the death of her father, the loss of their fortune and their relocation to Bath, she has held steadfast in the opinion that true love will be found. Can she find it right beneath her nose?

Hugh Baxter was rather irritated when his father asked him to keep an eye on his deceased best friend's daughters. But Lady Lily soon becomes a close friend and ally, especially during the Bath season - a dangerous time for any unwed man.

In the elegance and glamour of the season, will Lily and Hugh realise that their feelings for one another are more than platonic?

Printed in Great Britain
by Amazon

21658412R00088